The Lost Ones

Books by Walter Cummins

Story Collections
Habitat
The Lost Ones
The End of the Circle
Local Music
Where We Live
Witness

Novels
A Stranger to the Deed
Into Temptation

Nonfiction
The Literary Traveler, with Thomas E. Kennedy
Programming Our Lives: Television and American Identity,
with George Gordon
Managing Management Climate, with George Gordon
Florham: The Lives of an American Estate,
with Carol Bere and Samuel Convissor

Edited
The Book of Worst Meals, with Thomas E. Kennedy
Writers on the Job, with Thomas E. Kennedy
Shifting Borders: East European Poetry of the Eighties
The Other Side of Reality: Myths, Vision & Fantasies,
with Martin Green and Margaret Verhulst

www.waltercummins.com

THE LOST ONES

Stories by

Walter Cummins

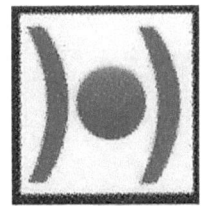

Del Sol Press
Washington, D.C.

The Lost Ones
Stories by Walter Cummins

Published by Del Sol Press
Washington, D.C.

Cover design: Walter Cummins

Author Photo: Minna Proctor

Printed in the United States of America

ISBN 978-0615659008

"You live badly, my friends. It is shameful to live like that."

—Anton Chekhov

For Alison,
who found me

Acknowledgments

Original versions of these stories appeared in the following publications:

"Another Person," *InkPot*; "Incomplete," *Midland Review*; "Nowhere," *Serving House Journal*; "Roxanne's Ride," *The Panhandler*; "Secrets," *Blue Moon Review*; "The Lost Ones," *Serving House Journal*; "The Way It Isn't," *PIF*; "Host," *Coe Review*; "Dreaded," *Perigee*; "Night Sounds," *Apocalypse*; "Saving Cimini," *Potpourri*; "Little Life," *Perigee*; "Awaiting the Night," *Conspire*; "The Dream Vatican," *Kansas Quarterly*; "Power Failure," *The MacGuffin*; "Someone to Clean," *South 85*

Thanks to

Alison Cummins, Michael Neff, Duff Brenna, Thomas E. Kennedy, Victor Rangel-Ribeiro, Renée Ashley, René Steinke, Jack Smith, Two Bridges Writers' Group

Contents

Another Person

The summer after his mother died Philip took a job as a busboy at an island inn that catered to the wealthy. He had never in his nineteen years known people who could spend weeks under beach umbrellas watching the roll of the surf. This job would help Philip earn tuition money needed for his sophomore year now that his father had so many medical debts. He had discovered the employment flyer on a dormitory bulletin board. After his application was accepted, it took him days before he could tell his father, certain he would be expected to spend the summer in a house shadowed with absence. But to Philip's relief the man just nodded and said it would be good for him to get away after all that had happened. And here he was, in a place he had never heard of, among people whose lives he would never have thought to imagine, his days devoted to gathering up their leavings while they pretended he didn't exist.

At college, though Philip had several friends for sharing meals and movies, he never told anyone his mother was dying, unable to think of a way to bring the fact into the conversation. The others just complained about roommates, mocked the professors, bragged how much sex they had and how little homework they did. How could he clear his throat and blurt, "My mother has terminal cancer"? A few times, very late, the hallway finally quiet, talking in whispers with people who had turned serious, admitting to fears of failing courses, of humiliating dates, of dismal futures, he had come close to speaking, then stopped, suddenly unsure that his mother was really ill, wondering if her cancer was something he had dreamt, not happening at all; that the next morning he would awake in shame and have to tell the others he had made it up.

Each day at the inn was the same: out of bed at six to serve breakfast, the sweet odor of the morning rolls already filling the dining room when the staff arrived; a break from ten till noon; a buffet lunch on the deck; a few hours on the beach before dinner; then set the tables for the next morning and step out into an evening crisp with salt air. Philip lived in a cottage with the other busboys, across the path from the waitresses' cottage, the young women chaperoned by the sour woman who supervised housekeeping at the inn. A week into the summer Philip realized none of the others really needed the money from their jobs, planning to spend all they earned on clothes or cars or electronic gear.

He roomed with someone called Terry and they got along well. Terry had a pleasant musical voice, offering continual anecdotes about life at his college, never telling the same story twice, always amusing, fun to listen to. When Terry started dating Theresa, Philip began taking long walks alone each evening, barefoot on the hard, wet beach sand, moving far from the lights of the inn to a spot where stars glittered in an endless sky. He would think how slowly the days passed, how long this summer seemed, how he felt trapped in time.

For Philip living his life was like watching a movie he had entered late, unsure how much he had missed, bewildered by the plot, seeing the actors move and hearing them speak, but having no idea what any scene meant, how it related to what had gone before and led to what would happen next. Every time he caught his reflection in a window he would think, That's me, as if the image were another person, someone who ceaselessly followed him, annoying in his constant presence, near enough to touch but always elusive.

One afternoon when Terry asked him what he planned to

major in, instead of saying that he didn't know, Philip found himself telling how his studies confused him. Everything was like the term paper he had written for freshman composition, the topic printed on a slip of paper literally pulled from the instructor's hat: General Gordon in Khartoum. He had spent hours in the library, retrieving dry books from grey metal shelves, taking notes, clumsily organizing the material, and receiving a C. All the time he kept thinking, Why am I doing this? What does knowing about a useless general in a country that no one cares about have to do with being in college? The instructor was a fair-skinned young man with thin blonde hair; the others ridiculed his pink scalp, and most plagiarized their papers. Terry shook his head and said they were fools; he was going to law school and you had to know how to do research.

Philip could talk to Theresa because she was Terry's girlfriend, but he was shy with the other waitresses, especially with Lucy, even though she was less attractive than most, short with thick, muscular calves, wiry brown curls, and a broad pug nose. Of all the waitresses she seemed most attainable, the one who might be willing to go out with him. But when he moved his towel close to hers in the group on the beach, she didn't interrupt her conversation to acknowledge him, and he never asked her.

Terry told Philip that his older sister was a corporate lawyer, very successful, always flying to London and Rome and Zurich. It was past midnight, the two of them lying in the glow of a bright full moon that filled their room. She was his role model, Terry said, and he meant to do something important too, something that mattered in the world. He was very proud of his sister, and he wanted people to be proud of him. He was much younger than she, born when his mother was in her forties, his sister already a teenager. Philip started to remark on the coincidence; though he had no sister or brother, he too had an older mother. But before he spoke he realized that he would have to explain that his had just died. Instead he told Terry he was an only child.

11

"I wish you could meet my mom," Terry said. "All my friends think she's great. So do I. So full of life. So enthusiastic. They invite her to parties. They tell me how much they love her. But I let her know I love her the most."

Philip felt himself redden, embarrassed at the expression of emotion, even though it was coming from someone else. Near the end, when he stood over his mother's bed and tried to tell her that he loved her, the words caught in his throat. Her eyes had seemed so far away.

He pictured son and mother together, sharing the same broad smile, the woman as outgoing and appealing as her son, and he suddenly envied Terry. "Yes," he nodded. "I'd like to know your mom."

For the final weeks of her life, Philip's mother had been discharged from the hospital because nothing more could be done for her. She lay between railings on a white metal bed installed in the large bedroom she had shared with his father, a plastic bag on a wire rack dripping clear fluid through a tube injected into a wasted arm, another tube collecting green bile from her nostrils. His father had moved into his room, and Philip, home from college for the holiday break, slept on the sofa; in fact, he spent all his time there, day and night, unwilling to turn on television, unable to read, hearing the visiting nurses speak to his mother, their voices muffled from behind the door, more a blur of sound than words. He would liked to have gone outside but didn't want to be seen by the neighbors and have to listen to their awkward sympathy. No one knew what to say to him, and he didn't know what to say to them.

Allen, Philip's best friend from high school, came to visit. Philip hadn't called him, but he showed up anyway, standing on the front porch with an arrangement of flowers in a plastic pot. It struck Philip as odd to see his friend holding flowers. "For your mother," Allen said. Philip rarely went into her room now, unwilling to see her so emaciated, jaundiced flesh drawn tight across the bones of her face. But he tapped lightly and opened the door to ask if she wanted to see Allen. Stretched flat in a darkened corner, she could barely nod. Philip stood back while Allen stepped toward the bed and told her that he had brought flowers, that he hoped she'd be well soon, his voice shrill, the sound of him overwhelming that still space. Then he turned and Philip saw the look of horror, the shock in his eyes, the mouth clenched as if he wanted to scream. Back in the hallway Allen touched Philip's arm once and was gone from the house, fleeing.

When his mother died, Philip was dozing on the sofa even though it was mid-afternoon. He sat up at his father's shout, shocked awake. His father plunged down the stairway, wailing, a fierce lamentation, like cries of a wounded animal. He seized Philip, crushing his body against him, shaking with grief. Philip stared over his father's shoulder, gaze fixed on a stain in the wallpaper, eyes burning.

One evening Philip was the last one to leave the dining room, inserting breakfast napkins into the juice glasses, their edges protruding like petals of a flower. When he closed the door to step from the inn, he could hear the whir of the refrigerator units and the rumble of the dishwashers; but outside the night was quiet. He moved to the front of the building, and when he saw no guests on the deck, sat in a web chair to watch the moonlight on the waves. Then he heard laughter, female voices—"He didn't!"—and more laughter. Theresa and Lucy moved across the deck, barefoot in shorts but wearing bulky cotton sweaters. Philip in shirtsleeves was shivering, trying to lean back into the shadows before they saw him. Theresa's greeting was friendly, and she sat in a chair across from his, Lucy beside her. Who did what? he wished he could ask, wondering what they would answer.

Theresa spoke first: "It's chilly tonight." Then Lucy said, "Aren't you cold?" He shrugged. "I'm all right." Theresa looked at her watch. "Oh, my gosh. I told Terry I'd meet him." Then she was

13

gone and Philip alone with Lucy, waiting for her to get up and leave too; but she did not move, and he didn't know what to say, the voice in his head cursing his silence.

"Do you like it here?" she finally said. "Sure. Why?" He couldn't see her eyes in the darkness. "You don't seem to be enjoying yourself." "I'm all right." He stared down at the boards of the deck, clamping both hands on his knee to stop his leg from trembling, a cool sweat spreading over his back; he clenched his teeth until she said goodnight and left.

The next morning when Philip awoke Terry was not in the room and his watch said almost seven. He had overslept, would be late, annoyed with Terry for not waking him. He threw on the clothing from the previous night and swished toothpaste in his mouth. When he reached the dining room, the others, the waitresses and busboys, seemed agitated, and he didn't see Terry. Bewildered, he moved to stand at his station although it would be ten minutes before the first guest arrived.

Through a window, out on a walkway, he noticed Terry carrying a suitcase, close to him, her arm over his shoulder, an attractive woman in dark glasses. His sister, Philip thought. Why was his sister here? A harsh wind from the ocean tangled their hair, rippled their clothing against their bodies. The two of them stood looking out at the sea, then turned and walked back toward the pier across the island.

In seconds, Theresa stood beside Philip, clutching his arm, her eyes glistening. "Don't you know what happened?"

Philip shook his head.

"Terry's mother died." She seized his hand, locking her fingers in his.

"When?" He felt numb, not sure this was really happening.

"Last night."

"When I went to sleep he was still out. He wasn't there this morning."

"His sister came in the middle of the night. They're leaving now."

Philip realized how much he liked the warmth of her, the touch of her body against his arm, and he blushed at his reaction but wouldn't pull away. "He never told me she was sick," he said.

"She wasn't. It was her heart. Absolutely sudden."

He imagined the woman sprawled on the floor, eyes staring, mouth agape, her son standing above her, crying out in his grief, and a sheet of blackness struck Philip like a blow. He staggered backwards, breaking free of Theresa, and ran through the dining room, down the steps to the employee toilet.

He slammed the door, fell against it, breathless, fingers trembling on the bolt until he could slide it tight. Then he turned and braced his hands on the cool white sink. When Philip looked into the mirror and saw the sorrow in his eyes, it was a person he knew. At last, he let himself mourn.

Incomplete

Gary almost missed the house even though he was creeping down the street in first gear. It was set far back on a narrow yard, obscured behind a tangle of untended hedges, a one-story converted summer cottage of white paint turned grey. The path from the street was cracked slate, weed clumps sprouting in the fissures. Toys littered the parched lawn—plastic rifles, a soggy teddy bear, a rusty tricycle upside-down on its handlebars.

The door to the screened porch was unhooked. Gary stepped inside, looked for a doorbell, and ended up rapping his knuckles on a pane of glass; then he held his breath, telling himself not to panic when the door opened and he stared into the man's face. But it was a pale young woman, barefoot in frayed jeans and a food-smeared sweatshirt, a whimpering infant held against her chest, a toddler in a soiled diaper clinging to her leg.

"Yes?" she said, eyes darting out past him. Gary shoved his hands into his pockets to stop their shaking. "I came to see my father."

For an instant, when her face went rigid, he thought the woman would hit him; but she sank against the doorframe and heaved with sobbing.

At twenty-five, Gary still looked like a teenager, raw and gangly, as if he had not reached full growth, wearing the same clothes his mother had bought when he started his first college. Since then he had been full-time in two others, part-time in three, and still hadn't accumulated more than fifty credits despite owing thousands in student loans. Most of his courses were pending with incompletes because he hadn't written a paper or taken a final. Sometimes after a night of cramming he would freeze at the door of the examination room, watching the instructor pass out bluebooks to his classmates, and then turn away, unable to step inside. Now, flunking a four-course load, he told himself that all he needed to break the inertia of his life was just one conversation with his father, a man chased out by his mother when Gary was eight and glimpsed only once since, years later, standing at the edge of a soccer field embracing a woman younger than his daughters, the memory familiar as the photo Gary hid in a drawer.

This woman, Gary thought, though the one back then had been bleached blonde and slender, laughing, lips thick with gloss, holding a cigarette in one hand, reaching the other to the back of his father's head and seizing his mouth in a lingering kiss. From the field, trying to concentrate on his position in the midfield, Gary knew his mother was seeing them too, that his father was putting on a performance for her. Now the woman, not yet 30, was drab and sagging, the baby crying with her, the two of them sniffling and red-faced while the toddler stared up with his thumb in his mouth.

Then she stopped, wiped a sleeve across her eyes, and stared at Gary. "I knew the second you got out of the car. One of Teddy's sons."

"Why? Do I look like him?"

She shook her head. "We used to watch you."

"How? When?"

"He'd park on the street across from your house when it was dark and look in the picture window. At you, your brother, your sisters, your mom."

"Why?"

"To see his stolen kids."

Gary shrugged. "He had visiting rights."

"With somebody standing guard. Never alone. Because she swore to the judge that Teddy couldn't be trusted."

Gary had a memory of being six, crouching in a corner of the room he shared with his older brother while his mother and father screamed at each other, then his father kicking open the door and hoisting him over his shoulder, leaping down the steps to the living room, and swinging him by his ankles. His mother beat at his father's back, tore his shirt. His father shouted that it was only a fucking game. But she sank her teeth into his father's shoulder, and the man dropped him. For a second, the world went black; then a door slammed and his mother swept him up. He had nightmares for years, even after his father left for good, waking up in terror, his brother slapping at him to calm down.

"When will he be back?" Gary asked the woman.

Her face collapsed, and he thought she would cry again; but she turned the expression into a grimace. "Never."

A slick sweat chilled his skin. It had taken him months to track down this address, weeks to work up the courage to come. He had barely slept the last three nights.

Gary hadn't told anyone his plan, not his brother and sisters, certainly not his mother. She would be furious if she knew, his sisters and brothers too, both for her sake and their own. Their father was a forbidden topic, and the others were thriving, Tom and Ginny and Lisa married with their own kids and their own houses. And his mother, looking terrific after a facial tuck, finally making money in real estate, had Mr. Gurston, his old high school soccer coach, a tall, bald man who ran marathons, newly divorced, still renting an apartment but spending most nights with her. The man used to growl at Gary's mistakes, call him by his last name—Knott—as if it were a curse, until he met Gary's mother and started acting like a buddy. But never, not on all the mornings they met in the kitchen, the man in his bathrobe, did Gary call him Richard. Always Mr. Gurston.

"How do you mean never?" Gary finally said to the young woman.

"Never—like in disappeared. No calls, no letters, no money. The morning after I told him I was pregnant with Jamie." She nuzzled her face to the baby. "Like it was my fault."

"How long ago was that?"

"More than a year."

The toddler was grinning up at him. Gary reached his hand down to his head and touched damp curls. It struck him that this boy was his half-brother. "What's his name?"

"Kyle."

"Yours?"

"Polly."

He said, "I'm Gary," and shook her hand.

She looked at his long fingers wrapped around her palm. "I guess I'm your stepmother." He thought she would laugh, but her eyes were bewildered.

"He married you?"

She pulled her hand away and started to weep again.

Polly backed away from the door. "You'd better come in." She led him past a wooden drying rack spread with diapers into a kitchen of grease-streaked enamel. Dishes were stacked in the sink, in the drain rack, pots on the stovetop. "I used to be neat," she said. "I used to give a shit." Kyle tugged at the refrigerator handle and swung the door wide. "Joos," he called. "Joos, joos, joos." Polly rinsed a glass and poured from a carton.

"Would you like something?" she asked Gary. "A beer?"

"I don't drink."

"Not a chip off the old block?"

"None of us drink. Except my mom. She likes white wine."

"That's probably what drove Teddy away."

He met her eyes, trying to tell if she were serious. "And what did you do?"

She stared back. "Spent too much time taking care of a kid. Then told him about another."

And got fat and sloppy, Gary thought. She wasn't really fat, just thick in the middle, a look that annoyed him. His mother was trimmer at fifty-five. And Polly was a woman who had to be at her best to seem attractive; her features were small and soft, the kind that peaked in youth, then turned to mush. It bothered him that his father had started with someone like his mother and then picked up with a Polly. "I thought he liked kids," Gary said.

19

"You four. Once. 'I had goddamn kids. What good did they do me?' That's what he shouted, and then he was out the door."

"Why'd you marry him?"

She lifted Kyle into her lap, wiped his mouth with her sleeve. "Because of this one. We'd been living together five years, and it didn't matter. But when the kid came, I made him."

"How come you lived with him in the first place?"

"Meaning because your mother had enough sense to kick him out that I must be stupid."

Gary shrugged.

"I was eighteen, night clerking in a 7-11, sharing a bedroom with two kid sisters, dating an asshole. This older man comes in for cigarettes and starts flirting with me. He comes back. Next thing you know I packed a suitcase."

"Look at them!" Gary remembered his mother's outrage at the end of the soccer match, he sweaty and panting, socks down at his ankles, craving a shower; she seizing his shoulders and shaking him as if his father's being there had been his fault; his sister Lisa hanging back beside her, head down in embarrassment, sneaking looks to see if any friends were listening. "Did you tell him about this game?" his mother had demanded. Gary had protested: "It's in the papers. Anybody can come."

"He had no right to bring that tramp out in front of my children," she said.

Though he said nothing, Gary had understood the man was trying to get revenge with a public display. He hadn't realized he was just being pathetic. Would he flaunt Polly in front of his first family now? No chance.

"Have you been looking for him?" Gary said.

"I ask around."

"And what do people say?"

"A neighbor saw him with a woman."

"In town?"

"Miles from here. He was fishing up in the mountains."

"Another teenager?"

"He couldn't tell anything. She was ducking into Teddy's car."

"Do you really want to find him?"

"Somebody's got to support these kids. I'm sick of the public assistance lady sneering at me." She lifted half the sweatshirt and guided a nipple into the infant's mouth. Gary turned away from the eager sucking. "What about you?" she said. "What did you come for?"

"There're some things I have to find out."

"Like what?"

He shook his head. "I don't know."

Polly had Gary hold the baby, Jamie, while she took Kyle into the bedroom for a change. Jamie wriggled, kicked his scrawny legs out from under a blanket. Gary expected a scene, not sure how to deal with a tantrum; but the baby calmed and dozed against his shoulder, skin red and puckered, as if he had been scoured with a strong soap. Gary wondered what he was supposed to feel.

Then Polly came back and exchanged Kyle for Jamie. "This one," she said, "should be trained by now. But he misses Teddy, the damn fool. I guess he's going to have a fucked-up life." She looked at Gary. "All of us."

"Do you really miss him?" Gary asked Kyle when she was gone, thinking the boy wouldn't understand.

"Da da," Kyle said and wrapped his arms against Gary's neck, hugging him. As much as he wanted to get away from the smell, Gary did not break the contact. "Ok, brother."

When Polly came back into the kitchen, Gary knew all he had to do was put Kyle down, stand up, say it was nice to have met her, and walk out to his car, never come back again. She was washed out, beaten down, probably would have ended up just like this even if she'd never met his father. No brains, no skills, no looks, no future.

But he didn't get up, rubbing his hand on Kyle's back, hearing a giggle in his ear.

"He's ticklish," Polly said.

"Do you want me to help?" Gary said, regretting the offer even as he spoke it.

"Help how?"

"Find him."

"Sure. What've I got to lose? Except that he might decide to come back."

They exchanged phone numbers. Gary gave her his address in a dormitory two towns away.

"What next?" Polly said.

"Where did your neighbor see his car in the mountains?"

She told him. A lakeside bar called Buster's on a county road.

"I guess I'll start there."

"How much support did Teddy ever pay for you four?"

"Not a penny."

"If we're lucky, he's gone to the South Pole."

Gary's car needed a tune-up; it strained uphill through a grey mist. He could barely see the lake beyond the bobbing boats moored along the roadside. Buster's turned out to be easy to find, the lone bar for miles, a small room with ten stools attached to a liquor store. In mid-afternoon the only people inside were two old men in buttoned cardigans and floppy hats. He showed the picture of his father that Polly had given him to the bartender, a red-faced man with strands of hair slicked sideways across his baldness.

"Hey! Look at this!" The bartender held the snapshot out toward the old men. "Ain't that the guy who trashed Carlisle's?"

The men looked at each other, grinned, and nodded.

"What's that?" Gary said.

"A motel down the road. I don't know what him and this woman were up to. But they started throwing around furniture in the middle of the night. Breaking lamps, smashing mirrors. The troopers had to come in."

"Is he still there?"

"Naw. They kicked the two of them out that night. Lucky they didn't get run in."

"What was the woman like?"

"Not much. Grey-haired, bad teeth. For a while, they was here every night getting drunk and grabbing at each other."

"Any idea where they could be?"

"Them two? Anywheres. He's your old man, right?"

"No," Gary lied, "just a relative."

His mother fussed over a Sunday dinner, packed the house with Gary's siblings and their families. Kids kept running in and out the side door, slamming the screen. The two babies—Lisa and Tom's—crawled on the carpet, pulling knickknacks from the end tables. Gary had never realized how cute and healthy all the children were, how their outfits matched, how many toys they brought with them. But he could see a resemblance to Kyle and Jamie, mainly in the bright blue eyes. His mother's eyes were dark, and so were Polly's; all the children had his father's eyes.

Then Richard Gurston walked in to a flurry of greetings, kids clinging to his long legs, Ginny and Lisa kissing his cheek, Tom's wife, Helena, too. Gary's mother just smiled. She still pretended they were only friends despite all the nights he had spent in her room when her children still lived at home.

At the dining room table heaped with steaming serving plates, Gurston asked Gary, "You go out for any sports yet?" as if his unwillingness were a personal affront.

I'm too busy looking for my father, Gary wanted to say, trying to imagine their expressions. But all he answered was, "I work out in the gym. I guess I'm not a team player."

His mother shot him a look. He stared down at his plate, then thought to smile at her and shrug.

Though he should have been in a morning lab, Gary was hanging out in the lounge at the student union, poking a straw into the crushed ice of a soda cup and kidding with a girl, Jessica, from his history course. A soap opera flitted across the giant TV screen against the wall.

"When was the last time you went to class?" Jessica said, a compact girl with sleek blonde hair.

"I took a course like it at another school. It's just review."

"How come you're taking it again?"

"I had an incomplete. Story of my life."

"I used to save a chair for you. But I've given up."

"If I'd known that I'd have sat through the lectures."

"It's not too late."

"We don't have to go to class to sit together, do we?"

She pretended to be watching the TV. "I guess not."

Then he heard his name. "Gary? There you are. You didn't answer the phone."

It was Polly bulging in stretch pants and a tee shirt, scuffing along in flipflops. He could see Jessica bite a lip. "It's my stepmother," he said, hoping she would laugh. But she looked at her watch and got up. "I'd better get to the library." She nodded at Polly. "Nice to have met you."

"I found out something." Polly waved several slips of paper.

"Where are the kids?" he asked, afraid she had left them in the lobby.

"At a neighbor's. Don't you want to know?"

"Sure."

"Credit card slips. A bill came today. He must be using an old card. But he's still in the state. Look."

Gary sorted through them. The receipt from Carlisle's was four weeks old, but the others were more recent, a few restaurants and two motels, still up in the mountains but fifty miles farther north.

"Let's go now," she said.

"You want to come?"

"I want to see the bastard's face."

Finding them turned out to be easy. She wanted to drive, but when Gary saw the mess in her old Pontiac, he insisted on taking his car. They reached the most recent motel by early afternoon, not stopping for lunch, and the clerk had a forwarding address to a cabin back on one of the lakes. "There're very cheap this time of year," the clerk said, a gaunt man in a bright plain shirt.

Gary turned at a sign onto a narrow road that cut straight through woods of tall spruces. The lake appeared as a sudden clearing, the dirt road circling it crowded with cabins on narrow sandy plots, windows shuttered, propane canisters on the side of each building with barely enough room to walk between them. A few boats were still tied to docks, but most had been dragged up to the front yards and flipped upside down.

"There's Teddy's car!" Polly cried. She pointed to a maroon Camaro with oversized rear tires.

"Where'd he get a thing like that?" Gary said.

"Traded his van for it a few weeks before he took off. I should've known something was up."

"I thought he took off when you told him about Jamie."

"Maybe that was just an excuse."

The cabins on either side of his father's were sealed, heavy padlocks chaining the boats, bars across the doors. Gary and Polly stood by his car, each, he could tell, waiting for the other to make a move. "Do you want me to go first?" he finally said. "That woman's probably with him."

"I don't care."

"Do you remember how you came with him to one of my high school soccer games and made out in front of my mother?"

"Did we do that?"

"Yes."

"I don't remember." She twisted her fists in the cloth and tugged her tee shirt down against her slack torso.

"Let's go." He strode onto the path, not caring whether she followed.

The woman answered his knock, wrapped in a quilt bathrobe that swept the floor, grey hair hanging loose, red-rimmed glasses on the end of her nose. Gary saw the folds of her throat and thought she looked like somebody's grandmother, then realized she was his father's age.

"Who the hell's there?" His father's voice from behind a wall, unmistakable after all the years.

"The bitch," the woman said. "With some guy."

Gary forced the door wide with his shoulder and pushed past her, felt Polly close behind. The cabin smelled of something burned in a pan, a grey haze still lingering. Suitcases lay open on either side of the fireplace, underwear dangling from the mantel, his wide briefs, her tangled brassiere.

The man, his father, Teddy, suddenly stood in a doorway, shirtless, wearing only pajama bottoms, the waistband looped under his belly. His face and neck were tanned, but the rest of him looked ashen, his chest patched with hair greyer than that on his head.

"It's pretty Polly wants a cracker." He lurched forward and closed arms around her, trying to kiss her mouth as she wrenched her head back and forth. The other woman laughed.

They were both drunk, Gary knew, not sure what to do, why he had even bothered to come. But when he saw Polly's pleading face, he stepped forward and put his hand on his father's shoulder, forcing himself in front of her. "Dad," he said.

The man's blue eyes blinked. "Oh, shit! Which one are you? Tom? Gary?"

"Gary."

"I used to be able to tell you apart."

"That was a long time ago."

"Damn right it was."

"So what's this all about?" the woman said. "Some kind of reunion?"

His father broke away from Polly and slung an arm around the woman's waist. "This is Francine. We ran away together."

"What about Polly?" Gary said.

"First there was your mother, then Polly, and now Francine. The best thing about Francine is that she can't have any more kids."

"Sometimes mine send me birthday cards, and sometimes I think to send them cards." Francine kissed his father's cheek with a loud smack. "We all get on perfectly."

"Who's going to support the babies?" Gary demanded. "Kyle and Jamie?"

26

"Why don't you get your mother to do it?" Francine said, and his father laughed so hard he pulled her backward onto a chair.

Gary wanted to slap her and hit him, turn the man upside-down and bang his head against the plank floor.

Polly was tugging at him, her face red, eyes fierce. "Let's just go. Let's get away from this place."

Gary let her pull him to the front door, then stopped and faced his father. He finally knew what he had to ask. "Tell me one thing, Dad. Am I going to end up like you?"

"If you're lucky, boy," Francine said. But his father shook his head. "No. You're somebody else."

Polly was the one to close the door behind them. They stood outside on a concrete slab, and Gary let her collapse against him and cry. He could feel her tears saturating his collar.

Later, in the car, she blew her nose into a tissue wadded around her fingers. She sniffled and rubbed a wrist across her lips. "Was that what you wanted to hear?"

Gary shook his head. "It's not enough not to be him."

"Then be yourself."

"Sure. Who's that?"

On the drive back after an hour of silence, Gary asked Polly if she had any family.

"Not anybody who'd care."

"So what will you do?"

"Food stamps. Get a job standing behind some counter. Day care at the Salvation Army."

"Then find somebody else."

"Who could somebody like me find?"

"Francine did."

"Yeah. Another Teddy. No thanks."

The next Sunday at his mother's family dinner, Gary deliberately came late, circled the block until he saw the cars that meant Tom and Ginny and Lisa and their families had arrived. Then he parked. Polly took Jamie from the car seat, and he carried Kyle.

"She'll scream," Polly said.

"Do you care?"

"I've been through worse."

"These kids ought to know their family."

"It's your party, Gary."

Just as they stepped onto the walkway to the house, Richard Gurston pulled up behind Gary's car. Gary heard his door slam, the man's voice shout, "Hey!" But he didn't turn around. "Hi, Richard," he called, moving forward, certain that this day would mean the end of something.

Nowhere

Deep into an endless mountain tunnel, the rail carriage lights flickered and died into total darkness. Marina could feel Ellis's fingers rubbing her thigh, then when she would not react, slide up toward her crotch. Her first thought was to scream so loud the train would shake; instead she seized his pinky and bent it back till he gave out a yelp and hissed in her ear, "Bitch!"

When the lights came back, she thought the bearded man halfway down the carriage was looking at her as if he had seen it all. He may just have been staring out at nothing, but he definitely had been watching her at the station where the train route started as she stood off by herself, relived to be apart from Ellis and the others. A duffle bag slung over his shoulder, the man had followed her eyes as she gazed up at the highest peaks, awed by their jagged enormity, with a sudden realization that she had to do something grand to prove she wasn't as small as she felt at that moment. Perhaps the man knew that too.

Now Ellis pressed against her, pinching the flesh above her knee, trying to give her pain. He moved his mouth so close she could feel the spray of spit on her face. "Don't you ever do that again!"

Marina laughed as if he had said something funny, and it came out hollow, not what she had hoped. The others didn't seem to be noticing. They were really Ellis's friends, with him when she met him in a Paris hostel while traveling at the end of the semester. Now she was bored with them, annoyed with herself for having sex with Ellis. She wanted to experience Europe, retrace the routes of the Romans on a map from her history course, and all they wanted to do was smoke the dope they bought in Amsterdam. She had done that with them just an hour ago, huddled around a table at an outdoor café near the station. No more, she told herself. She wouldn't be like them.

Ellis was still gripping her leg. "You're a real asshole." She spoke just loudly enough for the others to hear.

"You didn't say that in the hotel."

"I was hoping you were someone else then," she said. "A huge mistake."

"You were lucky I let you pick me up."

She snorted. "I could replace you in the snap of a finger."

"Yeah, who with?"

"That man." On impulse, she gestured toward the bearded man, but now he wasn't looking in her direction, facing the window with his straw hat tilted over his forehead, shading his eyes.

"Him! He's an old guy."

"At least he's a man." And now she knew she had to do something.

The train was out of the tunnel, moving through an Alpine valley squeezed beneath looming mountains. When Marina stood, she realized how much it was vibrating, tremors up her spine. She took a step and stumbled down the narrow aisle, flinging out her arms when the train lurched around a bend, thinking she still might be a bit stoned.

She dropped beside the man on the slat wood bench and patted his straw hat. "I like the look of you," she said. "It's probably the hat. I've always been a fool for a man in a hat." She fluffed his beard with her knuckles, then leaned back and propped her leather boots on the duffle bag shoved under the bench in front. She could tell he was resisting the impulse to stroke the beard smooth, decided not to do it for him.

"It's the age of Jesus," she said, turning to him as if in the middle of a conversation.

"What is?"

"The city we're going to. Its two thousandth birthday celebration starts tomorrow. I thought everybody knew that." She

30

spoke in a jagged staccato, assuming a voice that wasn't hers.

"I didn't."

"Then you must be from outer space." She pursed her lips and emitted a Twilight Zone *do do do do*. "Or maybe a hermit down from a cave in the glaciers."

"Close," he said. "To both guesses."

Now just a few feet away, she saw that he was younger than he had looked from a distance, probably in his late thirties, his face soft, the cheeks sagging, flakes of grey in his beard. What struck her most were the sad, brown eyes. She felt sorry for him without knowing why. "So what brings you to civilization?"

"Pot luck. I've been on trains for the past two weeks. Walk into a station and jump on the first coach I find. Sometimes I don't know where I'm going till I get there."

"Where do you live, when you're not riding the rails?"

"Nowhere."

Marina brightened with real interest, as if she had sobered in an instant. "But you're an American."

"If I have to be anything."

"Can't you find a nowhere to call home?"

"Any nowhere is as good as any other."

"You're in Europe. This is supposed to be an adventure," she told him, really meaning it. "You're supposed to be having fun."

"I've misplaced my instruction manual."

He didn't laugh, but she did and tapped the side of her head. "Mine's in here, etched into my brain. I could give lessons." She fixed her eyes on his, but he looked away, unwilling to meet her gaze. She knew what she had to do.

"Come to the city," she urged. "Indulge in the festivities. Rejoin society. With me. I mean it." She crossed her hand over her heart. "Try to be happy."

"What about your friends?" He gestured toward the young people crowded onto facing benches at the front of the coach. She saw them as he must have—three men and two women dressed in shorts and hiking boots, all tanned and fit, following their exchange as if reading lips, Ellis openly sneering. "Won't they miss you?"

She reached out and closed her hands around his wrists as if clamping steel cuffs.

He looked at her closely. "You're serious, aren't you? You don't even know me."

She gestured toward Ellis and the others. "But I know them."

"I get it." He shrugged. "All right. Why not?"

There was still time for her to tell him she'd only been kidding, just stand up and return to Ellis and the others for the rest of the trip to the city, before she went off with a sad stranger. But she saw the look on Ellis's face, on all their faces, and didn't want to be with them even that long,

"I should know your name," she said.

"Leon. My name is Leon."

She wondered if she should be someone else but couldn't think what to tell him. "Call me Marina," she said as if it weren't her.

Her phrasing seemed to puzzle him. "Is that really your name?"

"It is today."

"And tomorrow?"

"We'll see."

She'd make this man a challenge. Just getting him to smile would be a victory. But she told herself there wouldn't be any sex. She couldn't even imagine wanting him that way.

Minutes later at a transfer station, Marina retrieved her backpack from a rack over the benches where the others sat, refusing to look at Ellis, just mouthing, "Goodbye." When she rejoined Leon, she told him to move into the aisle before her, holding a strap of his duffle bag as if it were a leash. She'd done it—showed Ellis. On the platform she studied the yellow departures listing and saw that the next train to the city was already waiting. "Hurry," she urged. "Let's get seats."

Leon pointed to the others now gathered around a horse-drawn cart on the cobblestones outside the station, stroking the animal's flanks. "Aren't they coming?" he asked her. She shrugged and motioned him to help with her backpack.

32

She spotted free spaces and he hoisted their baggage up to the luggage racks. Then they sat across from each other by a blurred window. Ellis turned from the horse to glare at them. She wondered if Leon could see he was furious.

"Am I an excuse?" he asked her.

"For what?"

"Dumping a boyfriend."

"Him?"

"Aren't you traveling together?"

"This is my adventure. Now it's ours."

When the train began to move, Leon took off his hat and laid it on the seat beside him. "You picked the wrong person for excitement. I'm a very dull person."

"I suspect you have a secret." After she said it, she wondered if she were right.

"Nothing that would matter to you."

"All secrets matter."

He looked away from her. Through the haze of the window, Marina could see small white boats crossing a lake, sunlight dazzling on the water. During the rest of the trip Marina ignored the scenery and talked about the places she had visited, the stories richly detailed, practiced, the details exaggerated, skipping Ellis and the dope, wondering how he would react if she told him.

At the central station in the city, Leon stood beside her in the waiting area, the duffle bag slung over his shoulder. Large signs for the anniversary hung from steel beams high above them, the number 2000 in garish colors. "Now what?" he asked her. She had a suspicion that he wanted walk away and find a train to somewhere else. But she wouldn't let him. She didn't want to be alone.

"We'll get a taxi. Drop off our gear at the hotel."

"What hotel?"

"One right in the middle of the historic district. I booked it months ago. How else would a person find a room for a 2000th birthday festival?"

Outside the station, she signaled a cab, a black Mercedes

33

diesel, giving directions in classroom German, watching as the driver threw her pack rack and his duffle bag into the trunk.

Sitting beside her on the leather seat, Leon shook his head.

"What's the matter?"

"I feel helpless, being led around by someone half my age."

"But I think you're a man who needs a guide."

He almost smiled. She saw a slight curve to his lips and wondered if she amused him, if he liked her, if he found her attractive. A few friends, girls, had told Marina she was, and each time she would go home to study herself in a mirror. She found herself tall and strapping, blue-eyed, fair-skinned; but something was off, perhaps hair the wrong shade of blonde, lips too thin, or eyes too close behind the rimless glasses. She wanted to know, at night in the hotel had almost asked Ellis. Perhaps she would bring herself to ask Leon.

The cab cut across a wide boulevard and took a route of side streets down into the old section of the city. As the vehicle crept through the crowds of people that spilled off the sidewalks, she caught glimpses of wooden stands and bright decorations— balloons, banners, draped bunting. The driver stopped in a small square amidst a tangle of alleyways and narrow lanes.

Marina tapped Leon's knee. "We get out here." She paid the driver, wondering if Leon would offer if she had given him the chance.

He slid off the seat after her and followed to a wooden door under a small hotel sign. The building seemed ancient, coated with yellow stucco, bricks exposed where chunks had broken loose from the foundation.

In the lobby Marina rang a bell on a dark counter top, and an elderly woman appeared from behind a thick curtain. "I have a reservation." She unfolded a letter of confirmation, not speaking her name. Leon was watching closely as she signed the registration card, but she blocked it with her free hand.

He carried both her backpack and his duffle bag up the two flights of stairs, bumping them on the worn carpeting of the steps.

"You'll have to let me pay the hotel bill," he said.

"I can afford it."

"How do you know I can't?"

"You're my guest."

When she unlocked the door and swung it open, he dropped the baggage on the floor and flexed his shoulders. The room was tiny, dull wallpaper covering buckled plaster, framed reproductions tacked at odd angles—cows standing on a hillside of wildflowers, snowcapped mountains behind. Marina hadn't specified when she booked, but to her relief, she saw two narrow beds separated by a nightstand.

"The first thing I want is a shower." She unstrapped a side pocket of her pack and took a plastic sack into the bathroom. She turned the handles full blast. As water splashed over her, she wondered what Leon would do if she came out wrapped in a towel. Step into the hallway? Keep staring out the window? But she appeared already dressed, in bright culottes, sandals, and a pink blouse with a frilly collar, her hair braided and swept atop her head, fixed with a silver barrette. "Let's join the party," she said.

"Let me shave and wash up a bit."

"I left the bathroom a mess." The mirror was steamed, the tiles damp, her tights and underwear draped over the shower curtain.

"I'll survive."

When Leon closed the door, Marina stood at the window looking down into the square, at the swarms of people going in and out of the small shops, lunching al fresco at metal tables, taxis and vans threading among them. Even though the window was closed, she could hear the life resounding from the nearby buildings, sudden surges of human voices, shouts, laughter, recorded music, slamming doors. It was good to be here.

When Leon was ready, Marina took charge of the room key, tossed it on the counter in the lobby. In the square, she tugged at his hand. "Follow me and I'll show you where the city started."

She led him up a steep cobblestone street, a narrow-stepped sidewalk at one edge. But they climbed on the stones, Marina

35

skipping ahead despite the steep incline, he sucking in deep breaths and plodding as if pain were twisting through his thighs. At the top they came into a small green park.

"Legend has it that the Romans founded the city on this very spot twenty centuries ago," she told him. "It's the highest ground in the area, with a view that would spot any invaders miles away. Ideal for a fortress." She gestured for him to follow her along the path to an edge of a bluff. They overlooked a river and the streets along the quay on the other side packed with people. A garble of music swelled into the air—Germanic oompah, Latin rhythms, rock and roll, opera.

"You must be a fan of the Romans."

She nodded, imagining herself posed in a chariot, swinging a sword, slashing all foes. "I've been following their footsteps. Ireland, Britain, Gaul, Sicily. Trophies of conquering armies."

Leon surprised her by jumping back off the grass onto a slate path.

"What's wrong?"

"I could be standing on a burial mound, Roman skeletons under my feet. Soldiers far from home. Dead from the follies of mad emperors."

Marina felt the emotion in his voice and realized it was the most he had said since she met him. "What could they do? They were in an army."

"Run away. Just leave their swords behind."

"Did you know the Romans tattooed soldiers to catch them if they deserted? Then they killed them."

"Maybe it was worth taking the chance."

Leon was being serious, his face grim, and she didn't like it. So she snatched the straw hat off his head by the brim and ran across the park. For a second he stood flatfooted, then ran after her. She let him catch up to her, but when he came close, jumped onto a bench, holding the hat high above her head. He leaped from the ground and came inches from grabbing it, then climbed onto the bench beside her and seized her around the waist. She had been laughing, but he wasn't. She quickly set the hat on his head and pulled away.

As Leon adjusted the hat, Marina ran from the park, down the hill, sandals slapping at the stones, moving away from him, winding through the crowds and turning into an alley that led toward the river. She stopped to look for Leon following her and saw no sign of him, wondering if she should be relieved. But there he was, standing in the middle of a wide bridge, a man bewildered.

She thought for a moment and decided to call his name, "Leon," waving to him from the steps of a cathedral.

In the square behind the cathedral, a Brazilian samba band performed from a tier of wooden bleachers, dozens of players in bright red shirts and green silk sashes, barelegged female dancers with high-piled hair shaking gourds and castanets, plump, dark-skinned, throwing themselves into the rhythm. Marina started to dance too, on the sidewalk by herself, emulating the women, tossing her hair so hard the barrette flew loose. Leon knelt on the concrete to retrieve it as people paused to watch her.

"Dance with me." She opened her arms and wondered if he would step toward her.

He looked down at his dark boots and tried to follow her steps, then stopped and shook his head. "I'm not nearly as good."

"Why should that matter?" She fixed her hair with the barrette, then reached back and pulled him after her. "So much to see. So much to do."

They walked for several hours, up and down hills, along the river, around a lake, through neighborhoods, Marina always finding something to be fascinated about—a doorway, flowers in the windows, the shape of a roof, an orange cat that purred and rubbed her legs. She spoke her excitement, curious to see if he would react beyond silent nods, frustrated that he didn't.

When the sky began to darken, deep shadows falling on the streets ahead, she checked her watch. "Almost time for the ceremonies."

Night seemed to be bringing out even more people, more

noise, crowds spilling onto the side streets. Back along the water they couldn't find another outdoor table and had to join the diners in a dim basement restaurant, the food lukewarm and bland. After a few bites, Leon just poked at it with his fork. Marina ordered brandy, swishing the thick amber in the snifter, inhaling deeply, sipping.

When an amplified voice resounded from the night outside, she gulped the drink. "It's started. Let's go."

Leon insisted on paying, unrolling bills stuffed into his pocket, Marina urging him to hurry.

So many people packed the street outside the restaurant they couldn't move for a view by the water, just stood pushed against a building. A voice blared from loudspeakers on tall white poles, announcing in a German so distorted by volume that she had to strain to understand.

"What's he saying?" Leon asked.

"He's reading a greeting from our President."

A great blast shook the city, then burst after burst, an explosion of colors soaring across the night sky. Marina cried out, "Oh! Look!" stunned when Leon threw himself down onto the sidewalk, burying his face in his arms, huddling against the foundation of the building. She kneeled beside him and placed her hands on his back, could feel him quivering, his voice screaming "No" over and over. When people gathered around him, she told them to go away, that it was all right, even though she had no idea if it was.

When more explosions sounded, a rapid series of bursts, she thought to lean down and tell him, "It's only fireworks." But he wouldn't open his eyes. The crowd in front of them gasped and applauded.

After several minutes, he pulled himself up into a sitting position and used his sleeve to wipe tears from his face. "Sorry," he said. "I couldn't help myself."

Marina stared down at him. "What was that all about?"

"I thought I was still in the war."

"What war?

"A war I hated. Nothing but bombs, blood, and bodies." He grasped her hand, squeezed so hard it hurt. But she couldn't pull away.

She sat beside him. "I sensed it on the train. Something about you was terribly wrong."

"So many broken children." His body was shaking, his eyes blinking wildly.

Marina brought her other hand to his face, touched it softly. "It makes me sad. I shouldn't be sad. Nobody should."

"You would have been better off staying with your friends."

She began to weep, taking her hand from his and covering her own eyes. "I didn't want it to be this way."

Marina wasn't sure how long they sat on the sidewalk, dozens of people passing them by, not even looking. Then Leon was calm. "I'm all right now," he told her. "We'd better go."

When he helped her up, she began to push through the crowds, rude in her shoving, not caring that people cursed her. Leon took her arm, slowed her and led the way, she just staring down at the sidewalk, surprised when he stopped and she found herself in the square outside the hotel.

Inside, he asked for the room key and followed her up the twisting stairway. A few steps from the top, she tripped backwards. He reached out quickly to catch her, placed his hands on her shoulders, and she slumped against him. When Leon unlocked the door, she flopped on one of the beds, kicking off her sandals and burying her face in the comforter.

Noise resounded from below, even with the windows closed, the latches pulled tight. The narrow streets were echo chambers, sounds amplified by the walls of the buildings. She heard shouts, laughter, people yelling back and forth, words in a dozen languages, some in English, a shrill woman: "Have you seen Freddy? Where's Freddy?" She couldn't tell whether the person was amused or hysterical.

When she looked, she saw Leon stretched out on the other bed, fully dressed, eyes wide open. "You shouldn't have to be like this," she told him. "Living nowhere. Go home."

"You don't understand. I can't. I never can. I'm a deserter."

She looked at him blankly, then grasped what he was telling her. "You ran away?"

"I was only in the reserves. Never meant to be a soldier."

"Oh, god! Did they tattoo you?" she asked without thinking.

Leon touched his head. "My tattoo is in here."

"Are they after you?" Marina began to pace about the small room, looking at the door as if agents were lurking in the hallway. "Do they still shoot deserters?"

"Rarely. Just prison. But I keep moving, never staying in one place."

"How do you live? Support yourself?"

"Somebody wires me money."

"Who?" she demanded.

She didn't think he would answer. But finally he spoke. "My ex-wife. She thinks she owes me because she got to keep everything else. Even our children."

"Your life sounds so horrible." Her face knotted into a grimace.

The noise became a din, a marching band playing right outside the hotel—trumpets, trombones, tubas, what sounded like a thousand bass drums, feet pounding on the cobblestones. The tune was John Phillip Sousa, "The Stars and Stripes Forever." Marina went to the window, looking down at what must have been a hundred marchers, half of them beating on huge drums, snaking through the alleys around the square but always coming back on the same tight route. An endless pounding vibrated through the night. The drumbeats seemed to be inside her head.

"No! No! No!" She heard Leon screaming. He wrapped his jacket around his head, squeezed his hands down against his ears, kicking hard against the mattress.

Marina stretched out beside him, pressing her legs against his until they stilled, wrapping an arm around his waist, murmuring sounds, unsure if he could hear them with all the drumming. She pulled the pillow over her head to muffle the banging, thinking,

Stop it! Stop it! Stop it! until she couldn't think any more.

She lay with him all night, neither of them moving. Hours later, not sure how many, she heard only quiet from the square outside. A hard rain pounded the windows. The fierce storm must have driven the marchers indoors.

She got up quickly to use the bathroom, wash her hands, and splash water on her face. When she came back into the room, Leon was huddled on the bed, the jacket still wrapped around his head. Marina stood over him and shuddered.

She opened her backpack and threw in the few items she had unpacked. Then she pulled back the door and slid the pack through to the hallway, floorboards creaking, her eyes fixed on Leon's hidden face the whole time. She paused in the hallway with the door cracked just an inch, waiting for him to react. But he lay unmoving, a shape beneath a blanket. She shut the door tight behind her, slowly, until the lock clicked.

Downstairs in the tiny lobby, she gave the old woman her credit card and said her friend was still in bed. Outside the rain was heavy, a steady deluge, the streets empty, the revelers sleeping off the night before. Whatever festivities had been planned for this day would have to be cancelled.

She hoisted the backpack over her shoulder and cut through an alley to an open square. When Marina emerged from between the building walls, she discovered, all alone, untended, two camels tethered to a railing. She moved up to the animals, close enough to reach out and touch them, but they ignored her, staring out blankly, jaws moving, rainwater streaming down the sides of their thick tan coats.

Marina wondered how they came to be in this place, a city so far north. For an instant she had a fantasy that they had been abandoned by Roman legions twenty centuries ago, the tattooed soldiers all long vanished. The only person out in the downpour, she moved toward the central station, rain lashing her face.

Roxanne's Ride

The night fascinated Roxanne, as if the bus were burrowing through an endless tunnel, more darkness than she had ever realized during sixteen years in a world of streetlights, store windows, and blinking neon. The quarter moon lay smothered by cloud, just a pale glow suspended at the edge of nothing. She wanted to tell somebody how strange it felt to be hurtling into the pitch black. But she didn't have anybody who would listen.

The woman beside her in the aisle seat snored lightly, mouth open, glasses slid halfway up her forehead, head bouncing on the high seatback. She had been silent for hours, hands clasped and lips tight, snapping a single word when Roxanne had asked her where she was going—"Home."

During the daylight, Roxanne had pretended to look out the windows behind her really watching the other passengers: the red-faced man with the week's growth of grey beard, the plump woman in black-laced shoes who reminded her of Mrs. Aumuck, her second grade teacher, the man in the plaid hat who winked at her and gestured with an eyebrow. She had laughed out loud and refused to turn in his direction for an hour although it killed her not to glance back.

She gave them names in her head—Greybeard, Old Lady Aumuck, Fruitloop, Twinkle, Stone Face for the woman next to her, Buzzard for the winking man—and made believe they were going to the same town, some boarded-up place in the desert they all would clean and paint and fix up new to live in forever. She would run the TV station, making up shows, singing, dancing, the way she did when she was six and her father laughed and clapped. When she walked down the street, everyone would call her name—Hey, Roxanne.

But now, staring out into the night, she couldn't help picturing her mother walking into the bedroom, kicking off her shoes and suddenly realizing that the top dresser drawer hung open, slips and bras spilled onto the floor, the lock broken on the hand-painted wooden Indian jewel box and the four hundred and twenty eight dollars she had pinched together for a new refrigerator gone.

Even now, hours later, her mother still would be cursing her— her smoking, her stealing, her sty of a room, her scummy friends, cursing her name. "Goddamn you, Roxanne! I'm glad you're gone. Just stay away and stop screwing up my life."

She wanted a cigarette badly but swallowed hard and squeezed both fists, resolved to stop, to make herself good. All the others seemed to be asleep now, slumped in their seats, faces slack, breathing long and slow. The fools were missing everything, the promise of the night. How could people sleep when they were heading someplace new?

At dawn Roxanne still sat alert. When the bus lurched over a series of bumps, she could feel the vibrations in her teeth. Her ears prickled with the unending whoosh of ventilation; she swallowed a thick diesel odor with each breath.

Then the bus pulled off the interstate and slowed to maneuver the curve of the exit ramp, tires whining on macadam. Stone Face's eyes were still shut, her mouth open. Roxanne hesitated with her hand an inch from the woman's shoulder and decided that no matter what, from now on she was going to be nice to everybody; she would do things for people and they would like her. So she touched her gently with two fingers. "We're stopping for breakfast."

The woman let out a sour yawn, shifted in her seat, and shielded her eyes with a forearm. Roxanne looked out past the matted grey hair and blinked straight into the sunrise. She had to squint to take in the layers of pink at the horizon. All around, on

43

both sides of the highway, lay acres and acres of furrowed black soil, between seasons and empty. The highest structure for miles was the DX sign at the truck stop; it must have risen a hundred feet into the air, with the word DIESEL in letters as big as she was.

"Why is everything so flat?" she asked the woman.

The woman settled her glasses on her nose. "Because that's the way God made it." She said "God" like a curse.

The bus slipped between the tractor-trailers parked askew on the blacktop, some with cabs tipped forwards, some with engines idling, sunlight glinting off chrome, everywhere the smell of diesel. The driver stopped amidst the cars near the square, squat building of the diner. That's all there was: the building, four gas pumps, and blacktop with rows of painted lines everybody ignored.

A half mile or so down the road a few whitewashed houses clustered together around a silo. Three cows stood by a wire fence, chewing, switching tails, studying the bus with great brown eyes.

Roxanne let the woman off first and slipped into the aisle between Greybeard and Old Lady Aumuck, smiling and saying "Thank you" to no one in particular, then shuffled toward the front of the bus with the rest of them.

As soon as she entered the diner, she got a deep whiff of sizzling grease and felt her innards churn. She hurried back to the ladies room and had only a short wait for a stall, then leaned over the toilet for five minutes but ended up just spitting a string of phlegm. When she sat to pee, she took the plastic pen from her bag and filled in a four-letter word until it looked like BOOK.

Back in the main room, she thought she could eat but found all the tables and counter stools filled. So she flipped through the listing on the jukebox, regretting all the CDs she had left behind. But here she played no tunes, sure the others would give her funny looks. Except for a few little kids, she was the youngest person on the bus.

Roxanne moved to the rack of postcards, glossy scenes of cornfields, tractors bailing hay, lean white farmhouses, a map of the state with cartoons of corn, wheat, hogs, and cattle inside its borders. She slipped one from the rack and saw that nobody was looking. It would be so easy just to drop it into her bag.

But she stepped to the cash register and asked the woman, "How much?" She clicked quarters against the glass top. No more stealing.

She glued the last stamp from her change purse to the marked spot and wondered who to write to. She considered scrawling "I'm sorry" to her mother but then remembered she wasn't. Her leaving had been her message. And not yet to Tommy or Molly or Karen or Chuck or Fran. Not until she had a room and a job, a return address where she could invite her best friends: Come see me, stay at my place, anytime.

When Roxanne looked again, two seats at the counter were empty. She took one and, moments later, the man she had named Buzzard slipped in beside her, straddling his stool as if mounting a horse. She pretended not to notice, even when he set his plaid hat on the counter near the sugar bowl and twirled it by the brim.

The waitress, a hefty woman with tight blonde curls, tossed coffee-stained menus in front of them as she rushed past balancing a stack of dirty plates on a forearm. Hungry as she was, when Roxanne imagined biting into anything listed on the sheet, her stomach surged with an oily taste. By the time the waitress came back with a "What'll it be," she still hadn't made up her mind and began to stammer under the woman's glare. "Let me see . . . Let me see . . ." Then she noticed the pie plates on glass-doored shelves by the coffee urn. "A piece of apple pie," she said with triumph, the first food she had ordered in her new life.

"Why don't you get a big scoop of ice cream on top," Buzzard said, and when she turned to him, he cocked an eyebrow and winked again, a man with red-veined sunken cheeks and a mat of brown hair that looked like plastic.

She let out a quick cackle. "I'll get fatter."

He scanned her up and down with rheumy yellow eyes. "You look OK to me."

"Sure," she said in a disbelieving tone she hadn't used since she was ten.

"How about it, mister?" The waitress delivered Roxanne's pie and snapped up Buzzard's menu. He grinned back with missing molars. "Four eggs over light and easy, sausage, and ham. A pile of toast and a pot of coffee. I worked myself an appetite sitting on that bus." He patted his stomach as if he weren't a scrawny man with wrists like doorknobs.

Roxanne took a forkful of sweet pulp and soggy crust.

"Name's Craig," he said to her.

For a second she wanted to make up something and then figured it didn't matter. "Roxanne."

"Pretty name."

"Sure." She looked up at their reflections in the steamy mirror, he with the hat on again and the red neck of a plucked rooster, she square-faced and broad-shouldered, breasts too small and too high, thinking again that she might have made a better looking boy.

He slurped coffee. "Going far?"

"Last stop."

"Long way to sit."

"Can't afford to fly."

"I like buses," he said. "Nice way to see the country. Meet people."

"Not the one they got me next to."

He threw his head back in silent laughter as the waitress set down his plate. He jabbed a point of toast in the yolks and watched them run. "Any friends where you're going?"

She nodded, pretending it was true.

"Boyfriend?"

"Maybe."

"Figured you would."

"Why's that?"

"Girl like you."

She glanced up at the mirror again. "What kind's that?"

"Kind that gets boyfriends."

"Sure."

"Going to get married?"

"Me?" She almost spit out a mouthful of pie. She didn't like Buzzard, but it was fun to be talking to him, better than sitting next to Stone Face and smelling diesel.

"What's his name?" Buzzard asked.

"Tommy."

Tommy was as much of a boyfriend as she'd ever had. They'd hung out together since she was twelve and he eighteen, almost always with the gang, crowded six or seven into somebody's car or smoking on somebody's porch, listening to tunes, parading up and down the aisles of stores, stealing, sometimes breaking things just to do it.

"Is he where you're going?"

She shook her head. "Where I been."

"Then why're you here?"

"He's coming later." She blurted the lie and then felt her face break into a wide smile as she realized that it might come true. Not just Tommy. Karen, Molly, Chuck, Fran too—they really would join her wherever she settled. All of them away from the old shit in a new place. She imagined the scene of meeting them at a bus station, her friends dropping their suitcases and duffle bags to lock their arms around her neck in great hugs. "Hey, Roxanne," they would say, all piling into her car to head for her place. "Hey, Roxanne." She laughed out loud.

"You're one happy lady," Buzzard said.

"Yeah."

"So what's this Tommy like?"

"Tall . . . thin . . . kind of blonde." She groped for a description that a stranger could accept, knowing that other people thought Tommy was weird. More skinny than he was tall, with huge dangling hands, pale, pimpled flesh, and brittle hair that seemed drained of color. A twenty-year-old guy who did nothing but hang out on street corners with sixteen-year-olds. Her mother hated him. She truly did.

"You got something going?" Buzzard squinted over at her.

47

"We're tight." Roxanne clasped her right hand over her left wrist. "Like that." And it struck her how much she took care of Tommy, how she gave him cigarettes and money, how she'd listen for hours to how his bastard, drunk father used to beat him with a belt. What would he do without her? She brooded down at the bottom of the empty coffee cup.

Buzzard tugged at her sleeve. "Driver's signalling. Wake up."

'Yeah. OK.'

"Want to ride next to me? Seat's empty."

She looked up into his blood-streaked eyes. "Sure," she shrugged. "Why not?"

Roxanne wanted to stick out her tongue, wiggle thumbs in her ears. She could see the others sneaking looks at her sitting next to Buzzard. Stone Face seemed to take turns between glowering at her and scowling up at her canvas duffle bag jiggling in the overhead rack. Roxanne had spent hours decorating that bag with felt tips, marking both sides ROXANNE in letters that burst into multicolored flares.

Buzzard tapped his foot as if listening to a song. He wore scuffed black pointy-toed shoes crusted with mud.

"You like music?" she asked him.

"Got a transistor radio in my suitcase."

"What kind you like?"

"Loud. The louder the better."

"Rock?"

"Long as it's loud." He winked at her.

He seemed to be winking every thirty seconds since she sat down. But Roxanne couldn't tell what those winks meant, the way she felt when everybody else was laughing at a joke she didn't get. Buzzard's eyes were crinkled, his narrow mouth warped in a grin as if he thought they were sharing a secret. Still it was better than sitting beside Stone Face and listening to her teeth rattle.

"Where you going?" she asked him.

"Ain't made up my mind yet."

"When will you?"

"When I see someplace I like."

"How could you know you like it with the bus moving so fast?"

"Then I guess I'll just have to keep riding."

She grinned back at him, liking him a little now for his game of banter. If they could keep it up, the day would fly and they'd be somewhere. Night riding was best. The day was nothing but looking at cornfields and counting telephone poles. "Where's your home?" she said.

"Wherever I'm at. Right now this bus's my home."

"And when you find a place you like, will that be your home?"

"You got it."

"How long you stay in one place?"

"Till I get tired of it."

"How much time that take?"

"Sometimes a couple of hours. Sometimes a month. Sometimes a year."

"Then I guess you don't have a girlfriend." Roxanne laughed, amused to be the one asking all the questions.

"You mean somebody like your Tommy?"

She nodded.

"Nope. Girlfriends are like homes. Whoever I'm with, that's my girlfriend."

"What if she's got a boyfriend?"

He craned his head in all directions, looked up at the rack and under the seat. "I don't see no boyfriend."

She thought of reaching into her wallet to show him Tommy, but stopped with her hand on the clasp. She didn't want any of Buzzard's remarks. Tommy wouldn't pose for pictures, always covered his face when he saw a camera point at him. But one time Karen had caught him when he was sort of drunk, slouched open-mouthed against the wall of Chuck's house, pressing an icy beer can against the side of his head.

Buzzard snorted, made a gesture as if he was going to punch her, but just grazed her upper arm with his knuckles.

"You was about to show me a snapshot of Tommy, wasn't you?"

"I was. But I forgot. I left his picture behind."

"If I was Tommy, I wouldn't want no girlfriend of mine to forget my picture."

"He's going to send me a new one. He's having it taken."

"Maybe you'll forget what he looks like by the time it gets to you."

"Never happen."

He rolled his eyes and smirked. "You bet."

Instead of being angry, Roxanne was beginning to feel sorry for Buzzard, a man with no home, no girlfriend, nothing but a crap radio in a suitcase and ratty black shoes, having to sit on buses half his life. And suddenly she wanted to weep.

"There's nobody in the world like my friends," she said.

All her mother did was bitch at her; the only sign she had a father were birthday and Christmas packages mailed by department stores. "I don't know were I'd be without my friends."

"You're here. They're there."

"Not for long," she insisted.

"You got this far without them."

"We look out for each other."

"Yeah." Buzzard wasn't smiling now. "I knew people like that once. They don't think about me no more, and I don't think about them."

"Me and my friends," Roxanne said. "We're different."

"How come you never call me Craig?" Buzzard asked.

Roxanne clamped a hand to her mouth and choked on her laugh, coughing and sputtering. He stared at her for an answer. "You don't look like a Craig to me," she finally said.

"What do I look like?"

"Like you should be . . . ah, Willie."

"Willie?"

"Why not?"

"What's a Willie like?"

"I don't mean all Willies are the same. But—to me—a guy who

moves around as much as you do should be called Willie."

"What the hell's wrong with Craig?"

"I never knew a Craig before. It's kind of a fancy name."

"Maybe I'm a fancy guy."

Roxanne looked at his neck and his battered hat. "Maybe." She sputtered again. All she could hear in her head was the sound Buzzard, Buzzard, getting louder each time. She clenched her jaws shut for fear it would fly out if she opened her mouth.

"Christ!" His nostrils flared. "What the hell do you know?"

She shrugged.

Buzzard looked out the window. Roxanne noticed the long brown hairs that grew thick in his ears and turned to the opposite direction, looking out across the endless fields to a farmer alone on a tractor. What a scary way to live. All by yourself in the middle of nothing. Streets and stores and lights—that's what she needed. She could hardly wait to get to where she was going.

"I bet he's a fag." Buzzard suddenly turned and put his face up close to hers.

"Who?"

"That goddamn Tommy."

Her impulse was to laugh. But she stopped when she saw his eyes. "He's not."

"I bet he's got a tiny little pecker." Buzzard wiggled his right pinky and left it dangling. "Like a goddamned bob-tailed puppy." He snorted and flopped against the seatback, pulling the white headrest cover loose. He wadded it in his fist. "The sonofabitch probably wears diapers."

Roxanne squeezed her eyes shut to fight the tears. She felt so sorry for Tommy. Instead of being angry at Buzzard, she hurt for Tommy, at how much he'd miss her. Oh shit! She didn't want to think about it.

"Why're you sniveling?" Buzzard's words were becoming slurred, like a drunk's, although she was sure he hadn't had a drop since they sat together.

"Don't talk about Tommy." She kept her voice soft and pleading.

"Can't he take care of himself?"

"No." The tears broke loose now. She didn't make a sound, but her eyes swam in tears. They ran down her cheeks into the corners of her mouth. She tasted salt; it burned into a sore on her lip.

The bus hit a pothole, springs bottoming with a great thump. She heard gasps from the other passengers but could not see past the blur of her eyes.

"That was some goddamn bump," Buzzard said, cheerful again.

"Yeah." She rubbed her sleeve across her face.

"What was you crying about?"

"You know."

"That! Jesus! I was just teasing." He spread a hand on her thigh, hot through the thick denim of her jeans. When her leg twitched, he gave a quick squeeze. "Can't you take a joke?"

What would happen if she screamed? The shrill piercing plaint that had terrified all the kids when she was ten. She imagined herself screaming like a siren and the others snapping their heads to look out windows, pretending they'd heard nothing, the driver peering hard at the road.

Her duffle bounced in the rack above Stone Face. She watched it pitch from side to side.

"I'd better check my stuff." She stood quickly and tried to step into the aisle, but Buzzard gripped her wrist and yanked her back down into the seat. "It'll be OK," he said.

He did almost all the talking now. Buzzard. The side of his face pressed against the seatback as he murmured toward her ear. His hand lay on the padded rest between them, an inch from her arm, ready to snap out. So Roxanne sat very still and nodded or shook her head when he asked for a response. Outside the window the sky was layered pink and purple at the horizon. If she looked ahead, all she could see was a dark strip of highway disappearing into the sunset.

" . . . and she says to me," Buzzard was telling her, "Craig, if you do that again, I'll kill you. You know what I did?"

Roxanne shook her head.

52

"The same damn thing all over again. Right in front of her. Did that bitch kill me?"

She rolled her head from side to side.

"Damn right, she didn't. She didn't do diddly squat. So I kicked her ass and told her to get the hell out. I didn't want no part of her." His hand squeezed shut until the veins quivered around the white knuckles. "Weren't I right to do what I did?"

Roxanne waited until he reached out and she felt the pressure of his fingers on her arm. Then she nodded.

"Knew you'd think so. We're two of a kind, ain't we, kid?"

Buzzard stopped talking to watch several men fishing in a creek by the side of the highway.

"What's asshole do?" he asked suddenly.

"Who?"

"Your fag boyfriend."

"Nothing."

"Nothing? What's he live on? His good looks?"

"He's not working. No sense for him now. He's going to be coming out to meet me." For the moment she believed that was the reason Tommy didn't work.

"I got a feeling," Buzzard said, "that he ain't going to be coming. That's it's all over with him and you."

She forced a laugh. "Why?"

"Cause he's there and I'm here."

This time her laugh was empty. "Sure. Big talk."

"I'll show you things an asshole like Tommy never even thought of." His hand covered the fist she balled in her lap.

"I've got someplace to go," Roxanne said. "People're waiting for me."

"Tell me another one. Only one's waiting for you are police hunting down another damn runaway."

She tried to pull her hand free, but he squeezed until her nails dug into her own flesh. She had to catch her breath.

"Do you know how old I am?"

"I've had 'em younger."

"You can't make me do what I don't want to."

"Kid, you'd never believe the things old Craig is going to make you do. For starters, you call me by my damn name." Now he bent her wrist back. "Craig," he hissed at her. "Say, Anything you want, Craig."

She clenched her jaw until she thought her teeth would crack. "Buzzard!" she called, so loud all the others turned toward the sound. "Your name is Buzzard!"

He dropped her hand in his surprise, but just as quickly pinched the inside of her thigh. "I'll kill you, bitch."

Roxanne reached her other hand, the one that did not ache, into the pocket of her jeans, slid the matchbook up to the opening, and folded back the cover. She bent one match down against the stricking surface, and, as she pulled the book out, snapped it with her thumb.

She tossed the flaring matches into a newspaper crumpled under a seat across the aisle. "Fire!" she screamed. And Fruitloop and Old Lady Aumuck screamed with her. "Fire! Fire!"

People were shouting, kicking at the floor, Buzzard too.

The driver slammed the brakes, skidding the ball of flame under Stone Face's feet.

Roxanne jumped up and ran toward the front of the bus, all the time shrilling "Fire!" With one hand she caught the strap of her bag on the overhead rack, then heaved against the door, tumbling onto the shoulder of the road, rolling off into the weeds.

For nearly a minute she held her breath, expecting the others in pursuit, then only Buzzard stomping toward her in a fury. But the door closed with a hiss, and the bus just stood there vibrating with a throbbing idle, its stainless steel glinting in nightfall, the tinted windows blacking out everything inside.

If the door opened again, she would drop her duffle and run into the fields. But the bus wrenched into gear and eased back onto the macadam. Roxanne waited until the tail lights vanished, then stood up and picked the burrs from her clothing. She started walking in the direction the bus had gone, farther from home with every step, shivering, feeling herself being swallowed by the night.

Secrets

When Paul reached the end of the tram line three miles from Elke and Kurt's village, Elke was waiting, parked in the cobblestone circle, the Opel's engine idling, the children waving eagerly from the back seat even though Paul knew they had no memory of him from the time they were neighbors in the States. Astrid had been only four when they left, Rolf two, the most beautiful children he had ever known, blonde, blue-eyed perfection. Their coloring was their mother's, but Elke was not beautiful, her forehead too broad, her eyes too wide, her skin blotched red as if she had just come in from the cold. Yet Paul found her pleasant and attractive, the jumbled syntax of her English charming. Smiling broadly, she reached out her hand in a firm shake. "Welcome to our land."

Paul expected a quick hug like the one she had given him at the airport three years ago the evening she and Kurt and the children returned to Europe. Now her formality disconcerted him, made him unsure why she had been so eager for his visit. All through the hours of the flight he assumed she had read a need for human warmth in his letters. "We will give to you a cheering up" was what Elke used to say when she tapped on his door, Kurt beside her with a bottle of chilled Rhine wine.

When he sat in the car, his luggage in the trunk, the children turned shy, sliding close together and lowering their eyes whenever he looked back at them, still beautiful, Astrid's hair in a tight braid down to her waist, Rolf's close cut. Paul spoke to them, making his voice singsong, as if that would help them understand: "I have presents for you. In my suitcase." Elke quickly echoed, *"Geschenken,"* and to Paul, "Their English, it is not so good, yes?"

The narrow road to their house took a series of steep hills, up and down beneath a canopy of tall, lush trees, Paul's stomach made queasy by the rapid winding descents. Through gaps in the branches he could see great mountains rising in the background. He had the sense of being totally lost, even though Elke knew exactly where she wanted to go, driving fast, slamming the brakes at the curves and then roaring off, her arms rigid as she gripped the steering wheel.

The village was tiny, three rows of houses, a few shops, and some large barns, Elke and Kurt's house on a side street, grey stone with a red tile roof, a mound of logs stacked neatly beside the patio, inside all dark, polished wood and tile floors, cool, bright tapestries on the pure white walls. "Very nice," Paul told Elke, disoriented, everything totally unlike his impressions from the photos they had sent.

"It cost more than we have money to afford," she said, as if the fact were amusing.

"But much better than your accommodations in the States."

They had lived in adjoining crackerbox townhouses for the two years of Kurt's American job assignment, a career move, a sign that Kurt had been singled out for rapid advancement. He was having a beer in Paul's kitchen when Elke arrived a week after him, but a day earlier than expected, some confusion in the flight plans. Paul watched as she pulled herself from a taxi, in the last stage of an ungainly pregnancy, then stood on the blacktop parking area with a suitcase in each hand, looking as if she wanted to cry, two-year-old Astrid clinging to her leg. Kurt had run out and swept up his daughter, swirled her, covered her face with a dozen kisses.

That was shortly after Paul's divorce, the townhouse temporary he had told himself at the time, though he still lived there, unopened cartons stacked in the storage closet. The walls were like cardboard. Then Kurt and Elke's muffled conversations, sounds in a language he couldn't comprehend, had made him feel less alone. Now his neighbor was an old woman who blasted her TV twenty hours a day.

Elke gave him towels and pointed out the downstairs bath, a small room bright from a wide, frosted window, plastic toys lined on the edge of the tub, a man's robe hanging from a hook on the door. When Paul came out, shaved and freshly dressed, Elke poured him a glass of white wine and they sat by the unlit fireplace, discussing his trip, the plane, the train, the tram, and then chatting about others from the townhouses, people they had known in common. The children sat on the rug, quietly listening, even though he knew this talk would make little sense to them even if their English were perfect.

When evening began to fall, Elke excused herself and moved into the kitchen, spoke softly to the children while she pulled pots from a cabinet. The children began setting the table, Astrid with the silverware, Rolf carrying stemmed glasses, tiptoeing with one at a time. Paul dozed while watching the purple glow of sunset behind the mountains, startled when Elke called him to sit down. At the table, he counted the settings and saw no place for Kurt; it struck him that she had hardly mentioned her husband the whole time they had been talking. He hesitated to question, not sure he really wanted to know why. When he did ask for Kurt, Elke shrugged: "I must make his apologies for him. Today is a day that he must work very late. His company, it is very demanding of his hours."

Rolf dominated the meal, speaking constantly now, his gruff voice incongruous for such a small boy, asking Paul many questions that Elke had to translate, Astrid giggling with each one: how big was the airplane? Did Paul live in Disney World? What was his favorite cartoon? "He has much curiousness," Elke said.

After dinner the children put on music, a CD of a solo flute, and they danced, Astrid in pink leotards, straining to stay on tiptoe, spinning, the long braid swirling with every movement. Rolf hopped up and down in one spot and shook his hips, Elke clapping soundlessly, trying to make them follow her rhythm. "It is their favorite thing, to dance," she told Paul.

Later, after the children took their baths and went to bed, Kurt still had not come home. Elke refused to let Paul help with the dishes: "You are to be our guest." He sat in the parlor listening to the rush of water, the clatter of china, again wondering why he was there. During the months they were neighbors, they had spent many evenings together, he at sea after nine years of marriage, Elke and Kurt strangers to his culture, eager to listen to his explanations; but Kurt eventually took so many business trips he saw more of the country than Paul ever had, returning with souvenirs and hours of digital video.

When the family moved back to Europe, they exchanged notes, holiday cards, photos of the children, and then came Elke's surprise call with an invitation to visit, urging him to say yes, assuring him that Kurt also would be happy to see him.

When the dishes were stacked, Elke took off her apron and joined Paul with a new bottle of wine. He expected her to ask about his life, a continuation of the conversation they used to have when Kurt was on one of his trips, Elke bathing Rolf in the sink, Astrid on his lap with a coloring book, he picking apart his marriage, reliving conversations, gestures, expressions as he sought the source of its failure. Elke had been a patient listener, nodding "Ja Ja" and telling him, "It is not so good for to blame yourself so much."

Now she sat on the sofa beside him and touched her glass to his, then looked across the room at the wall clock, saying nothing. Paul glanced down at his watch and saw the time. "Has Kurt been promoted?" he asked.

"I suppose so," she said. "We don't talk of such things. His work, it is very tedious. Why should I want to know so much about it?"

He couldn't tell if she were serious. "We used to discuss our work all the time in the States."

"That's because Americans have nothing else to talk about. You live to work. You think about only how important is your careers."

"But right now Kurt isn't here because of his."

"That is what he tells me is so."

In the silence, not knowing what to say, Paul poured more wine for both of them, studied the label, commented on the crisp, fresh taste.

Elke touched his hand, her long fingers covering his, and guiding the bottle back to a tabletop. "It's not so good with us, me and Kurt."

He nodded. "I've felt that since I arrived. Did something happen?"

"It is what is not happening. We live our lives like separate people."

"That's sad." Paul knew he should say more but couldn't find words. He was very tired—the wine, the long trip.

"I lie awake all night thinking about what could have been," Elke said after a silence. "The life I missed. The person I missed." She paused, waiting for Paul to react, continuing only when he blinked his confusion. "He calls me now. We talk. I called him once for the first time, after many years. And now he is the one who calls."

"What person?"

"My teacher once. My teacher when I was very young. He was the first man for to make love to me."

"A much older man?"

"Not so much. He wanted me to marry with him."

"Why didn't you?"

"I was still in school. I was so young. All I cared about then was to make love."

"And now?"

"I think about him always. All the time. The terrible mistake I made for my life."

"Is that why you called him?"

Elke nodded, her large pale eyes glossy with tears. "One night, it was very late, and still no Kurt. There was no moon, just darkness. The wind made the house to shake. I dialed his old number not even knowing if it was there he still lived."

"But he did?"

"A woman answered."

"His wife?"

She shook her head slowly. "No. Some person he lives with.

59

But I didn't care. I asked for to speak with him anyway. When I heard his voice, I cried." She started to weep now, but just sniffled, wiped her eyes, and smiled. "He calls since then. I never know when he will call. All day I wait for him to call."

"What does he say?"

"He will leave her, that woman, leave her for me. He wants for me to meet him in his city. He wants for to see my face."

"Will you go?"

"I don't know!" And now she burst into tears, fell against Paul, clung to him, her body trembling, her thick hair in his eyes. He stiffened, not sure what to do with his hands, then laid them gently on her back, patting and rubbing, wondering what would happen if Kurt walked in the door at that moment, thinking how a mistaken appearance could complicate all their lives.

"You have a husband," he said, "children."

"My husband, he makes me miserable." She cried even harder.

"You seemed so happy in the States," Paul said. "I was the miserable one. Just being with the two of you made me feel better."

"There we were in a different world. Everything was different." She pulled away from him and sat back, twisted her hair into a knot. "You must tell me what I am to do?"

"Is that why you invited me?"

"Yes."

"Don't you have anyone here to talk to?"

"Here people don't talk about such things."

Paul stood up, walked to the front of the room, and looked out at the moon, hoping Kurt's car would suddenly appear on the empty street. He remembered her advice to him in the past, all the times she had said, You are not so much to grieve. He knew he owed her words of comfort but had no idea what to say. "Elke, how can I make a decision about other people's lives? Look what I did with my own."

"If I go to him," she said, "look at him just one time, I will never come back."

"And the children?"

She shook her head sadly, the hair falling loose, covering her face. "I cannot leave my children."

"What if you took them with you?"

"He, my friend, lives poorly. He has no room for children. He wants only me."

"Then he gives you the choice of being a lover or a mother." Paul spoke slowly, as if analyzing a problem that had nothing to do with actual people. He realized he did not like this unnamed man, Elke's friend.

"Yes, I can stay here to be miserable with my children. I can go to there to be miserable without them."

"And Kurt? Isn't there anything you two can do?"

"No. Nothing." She gave him a stare of defiance. "Never."

Before Paul could protest, headlights swept across the wall and he heard the crunch of tires on gravel. Kurt was home.

The car door slammed, the house door opened; Kurt dropped his briefcase on the tiles of the entranceway and called Paul's name, grinning broadly, arms spread wide in greeting. He strode across the rug and, instead of shaking hands, embraced Paul. "My friend, it's so good to see you after all this time."

Kurt had a mustache now, and small rimless glasses, his thinning hair much wispier under the glow of the ceiling lights. When he released Paul, he leaned down and gave Elke a quick kiss on the top of the head. "What a day."

"I hear your company is overworking you," Paul said, trying to make a joke of it.

Kurt gave an exaggerated sigh. "You don't know of half of it." He hung his jacket on a coat rack, loosened his tie. "Life was much more manageable in the days we were neighbors."

"So you miss the States," Paul said.

"Some things. And some things are better here. And what about you? Is your life finally better?"

Paul shrugged. "I keep telling myself I'm on the verge of taking the next step."

"And what step is that, my friend?"

"If I knew, I'd be able to take it."

Kurt laughed loudly, as if Paul had said something very funny.

Elke asked him if he wanted his dinner, abruptly, not hiding her annoyance.

"I ate in the city with people." He saw the bottle on the table. "Some wine won't hurt." He waited for Elke to get a glass from a cabinet and pour for him. They exchanged words in their language, she abrupt, his voice rising. She handed him the glass.

"*Hier!*" and turned her back.

"And how have the children been?" he asked Elke after he sipped. Kurt's English was easier than hers, his accent less pronounced, though his vowel sounds had always struck Paul as odd.

"The children have been children all day," she said.

Kurt winked at Paul, as if they shared a secret. "And sometimes the adults are children," he said. "But adults must play too, isn't that so?"

Elke looked at him. "It is time for to go to bed. I am very tired from being an adult. And you should let Paul sleep too."

"In a few minutes. I've missed my friend." He raised his glass in a toast.

Kurt watched her climb the steps and raised his glass again, to her back. Then he sat beside Paul on the sofa, reached out to squeeze his arm. This gesture, like the hug, surprised Paul; Kurt had never been a toucher before.

"So, Paul," Kurt said, "you're still brooding over your divorce."

"I miss being married, and I don't like having made a mess of things."

"Perhaps it's impossible for our lives not to be messy." Kurt smiled as if the thought amused him.

"And what about your life?" Paul asked.

"My life is very messy and very pleasant."

"Would Elke agree?"

"I have no idea, my friend. The pleasant part has nothing to do with her."

"So the messy part must."

"A man shouldn't criticize his wife." Kurt tilted his head back and drained the wine.

For a second Paul thought he should speak of Elke's unhappiness, but sensed that would be a mistake now. Instead he asked, "What happened? You two were so close in the States."

"That was living in a fantasy world. We were the only two people who spoke the same language. She gave me a son. This"—Kurt slapped the wood of the table, pointed at the walls—"is the real world for us."

"You have a son here. And a daughter."

"They are two of my greatest joys."

"The source of what's very pleasant?" Paul said.

Kurt laughed. "In part. Stay here. I want to show you something, my friend." He crossed the room to retrieve his briefcase, snapped it open and searched inside as he returned to the sofa, lifting out a mailing envelope as he sat again. He looked toward the stairway as if Elke might be standing there watching, then pulled two photographs from it with his fingertips. Silently, eyes glowing, lips pressed into a smirk, he passed them to Paul.

Paul took one in each hand and turned them over. They were, as he expected the moment he touched them, of a woman. One photo was a close up of a young face under meticulously waved hair, the other a shot of the same woman in a lowcut cocktail dress, the shadow of her cleavage prominent, as if she had just taken a deep breath to thrust out her chest. Paul's first thought was that she wasn't any more attractive than Elke.

"So," Kurt said, touching the edges but not taking the photos from Paul.

"Who is she?"

"The people I ate with tonight." He broke into a broad smile. "My reason for putting in such long hours. A trial of my corporate responsibilities."

Paul placed the photos on the cushion between them. "What does this mean?"

"Mean? In what way?"

"Are you in love with this woman? Will you leave Elke?" Paul met Kurt's eyes and held his breath, aware that a simple "Yes" would change many lives. Elke would retain custody. There would be a settlement. She could force her old teacher to rethink their crisis. But Paul realized he wasn't sure he wanted that; he had no idea what would be best for these people.

"Leave Elke?" Kurt seemed shocked at the question. "Of course not. She is the mother of my children. It is very important that I be with my children."

"But what about her?" Paul pointed at the photos.

"I have great affection for her. She is a source of much joy. And she understands how it is for me."

"Do you truly love her?" Paul insisted.

"My friend, I love her enough to be happy." Kurt placed the photos back in the envelope, spread apart the clasp, and pressed down with his thumbs. "My wish for you is that you will be as happy also."

"Is it me?" Paul said. "My example that put you off the idea of divorce?"

"You? You have nothing to do with it. It's not like America here. There is no need for divorce. Not for something as foolish as infidelity."

Paul clutched the sofa with a sudden anger. "It was my wife."

"You Americans take life's games too seriously. Always in a hurry. The alternative is to let things pass with time."

"Not for me."

Kurt reached upward and yawned as he stretched, twisting his torso. "That was your mistake."

"What about Elke? What if your wife were unfaithful?"

"How would I know?"

"What do you know about her? Do you even know if she's happy?"

Kurt shrugged. "That's not something we talk about. I hope she is. Elke has her children. Why shouldn't she be happy?" He looked at his watch. "It's been a long day for all of us. Now that you are here, there will be much time for talk."

Kurt paused at the bottom of the stairway, briefcase in hand, and yawned again. Paul almost called him back, but the sound died on his lips. He had several days ahead to decide what he would reveal to the husband or to the wife.

Kurt snapped off the light when he reached the top of the stairs, and Paul looked out at the night, the shadows of tree limbs like cracks across the windows, the grey shapes of mountains in the distance. Above him he heard the creak of a mattress, Kurt lying beside Elke in the darkness. And he understood that he would not repeat a word to either of them, that he had been told these secrets because he was a man who could make nothing happen to their lives.

The Lost Ones

When she announced herself on the phone—"It's Libby, Libby Merchant"—the voice high-pitched, as if at the edge of hysteria, Roger remembered her immediately, the skinny girl with a head of tight brown curls, eager on every committee all through high school. He hadn't thought of her for years and wondered why on earth she was calling now. "It's our thirtieth," she announced. "Can you believe it?"

"Not really," he told her, shaking his head, wishing he could hang up.

She wanted him to help track down some people everyone had lost touch with. "You'd be good at that," she said, and he was sure she had no idea what he was good at. They'd hardly known each other. But, taken by surprise, it was easier to agree than come up with an excuse not to.

"We call them the lost ones." Libby emitted a nervous laugh, as if the loss were her fault.

"Who's on the list?" he asked and listened to her recite names of people he had no memory of until she came to Lauren Duryea. Roger didn't think his swallow made a sound, but Libby reacted as if she had heard.

"Weren't you two close?" she asked.

He imagined her eyes narrowing. "Briefly. A long time ago."

"Otherwise she wouldn't be lost." Libby laughed again. She promised to email him whatever details she had about the names and said an abrupt goodbye, clearly with many others to call for favors.

"I'm on a reunion committee," Roger told his wife, Evelyn.

"Hunting down lost classmates." She had been sitting in a chair on the other side of the room, listening to the conversation with puzzled eyebrows.

"I suppose that means we'll have to go." She sighed. He understood it would be an ordeal for her. She hated being confronted with new groups, content to socialize with a few long-time friends. "You never talk about high school. Why do you care?"

"Curiosity," he told her. "I want to see what happened to kids I grew up with, how their lives turned out."

"What really matters," Evelyn said, "is how *your* life turned out."

He walked across the room and stroked her hand.

Lauren Duryea. Over the years, Roger had played with the fantasy of a life with her, in the dark of sleepless nights recalling Lauren at eighteen, the deep grey eyes just inches from his, her fingers stroking his face, then kissing him with hungry eagerness. Roger could still feel the surge of her need.

But, even in moments of arousal, breathless, he had never told her he loved her, just that she was wonderful, precious. And she, in turn, only spoke his name, again and again, with such intensity that the memory of it, the sound in his brain, made him shiver.

They never had actually made love, though he was sure Lauren would have been willing, even more than he. They didn't even speak of it, the way he had with other girls, engaging in a negotiation inseparable from the act. He wouldn't think of asking if she were a virgin. Just the question would have been a violation. Roger had never had that feeling with another person, and the more he thought about it, he realized the issue hadn't been sex, the only thing he could name when he was young, but something else, something more profound that he still couldn't identify. He suspected that was why he had resisted consummation, as close as they had been to it, a mere touch away. Yet often, staring at the shadows on the ceiling, he had brooded, fearing a terrible mistake. If they had made love, his life would be different.

And yet they had drifted apart. No, he had been the one, choosing a college a thousand miles away, and while she wept, telling her it was because he had won a scholarship even though the award was small, merely enough to pay for books and fees. He had convinced himself that he couldn't turn it down. At first, he wrote several times a week, called her, then, gradually, stopped. She stopped too. Later, he believed it had been his decision, she stopping because he had.

With the list of lost classmates Libby Merchant had given him, Roger deliberately avoided seeking Lauren, giving himself time to ponder what he would do when he found her. He did his hunting at work, in the privacy of his office, entering names in his search engine, learning that some of the results gave ages. That's how he identified two of the men. The women were more difficult because of maiden names, but Libby had provided clues from others in the class, the vague memory of a married name, the states they had moved to. He was able to narrow down possibilities, sending emails and, after receiving several replies of sorry, not me, tracking down two more. They didn't recall him but remembered Libby. Everybody knew Libby.

Roger had seen Lauren once in the time since high school. Just weeks after he missed the tenth reunion, deliberately, not knowing what he would have done if she were there, Lauren called him at his office in a city five hundred miles from their hometown. He recognized her voice immediately, in his surprise blurting, "How did you find me?" She had laughed, telling him it was easy, a mutual friend, but wouldn't give the name, teasing him to guess. No, no, she kept saying with each person he suggested, shaking her head, and finally changing the subject.

"I was hoping to see you at the reunion," she told him.

"I couldn't make it."

"Neither could I. But it made me wonder about you."

He thought before answering. "That's nice to hear."

"Guess where I am?"

"Back in our town?"

"Hardly. I'm two blocks from your office."

Her own job, running training sessions for a large company, she said, had brought her to his city for a convention. Her evening was free. Could they meet? Roger found himself pretending to cough, forcing the words out. Of course he could. It would be great to see her. Then he sat for a half hour, his hand clutching the phone, trembling, before he could make himself lift it to tell Evelyn something came up. He'd have to work late. As usual, she didn't ask for an explanation.

Lauren reached out to shake Roger's hand when they met in the lobby of her hotel, then laughed and gave him a quick hug. He tensed, barely touching the back of her jacket, stepping away to take her in, nod appreciatively, spot the wedding ring on her finger, a narrow gold band. "You're looking great." Wonderful, he wanted to say. Spectacular. Incredible. "You too," she said, squeezed his hand, gave him an intense gaze that he told himself was a professional trait, wouldn't let himself believe was for him alone.

"I've reserved a table." He let her lead him into an elevator that rose to a rooftop restaurant overlooking the city. Despite the decade he had lived there, he had never been in this hotel.

When they sat, Lauren was still staring at him, mouth turned in what seemed a secret smile. Roger broke the contact and looked past her to the glowing lights beyond the wall of windows. It's a game, he thought. She's playing with me. But when he turned back to her, she was studying the menu.

To make conversation, he told her, "You certainly travel well." He gestured toward the room, the lighting, the chandeliers, the flowers. "Is this typical?"

"Hardly." She smiled openly. "I spend my days in a cramped office or a windowless classroom."

"And your nights?" The words jumped out of his mouth. He rubbed his face as if he could erase them, not looking at her hand on a wine glass, the ring reflecting candlelight.

"Our house is quite ordinary. Cluttered. All those toys the boys won't put away."

"You have children." He felt a sinking of disappointment, then relief. She was encumbered, could never be more than a fantasy, a creature in his fiction of an alternate life, someone else, not the real Lauren.

"Two boys. Six and four. With my job they spend hours in daycare."

Lauren opened her purse and pulled out a loose photo of posed children, boys, the older standing, the younger on a chair, the print in a brown tone, the paper stiff, like the photos that come with the purchase of a picture frame. Neither boy resembled Lauren. "Handsome," Roger said.

"Taken by a professional. I can never get them to sit still."

"What does your husband do?" he asked.

"Vic? Not much."

Roger's expression, the quick snap of his head, brought another laugh from her. Short, abrupt.

"I meant not much with the boys. His hours are longer than mine. We hardly see each other. Even weekends."

"Where did you two meet?"

"We were a college romance. You know how those go." She raised her eyes.

"Not really. I never had one. Just dates."

"So where did you find your wife?" She gestured toward his ring. He looked too, surprised to be wearing it, though he had been for almost four years.

"At my company. In another building. We were on the same mailing list."

"Ah, a corporate romance." She smiled again, and Roger doubted that she meant it. Despite the look on her face, her air of enthusiasm, he didn't believe she was happy, then wondered if that was only what he wanted to believe.

He risked a statement, squeezing an edge of tablecloth in his fist. "College and corporate. Both more substantial than high school."

For a second he thought she was going to reach out for his hand, but she just brushed something he couldn't see from the tablecloth. "Oh, we had our moments." He couldn't tell if her tone were genuine.

They disputed the check, playfully, Lauren arguing that she was on travel expenses, Roger that he wanted to treat her. She won by giving the waiter her room number while he sat with a credit card in his hand.

They were silent while a busboy cleared the dishes, still not moving when the table was empty. "Would you like another drink?' Roger asked her, knowing that he should have gone home an hour ago, that Evelyn was there, alone.

She nodded. "But let's move to the bar."

He pulled her chair back, standing close, breathing in the scent of her hair.

In the bar, Lauren did most of the talking, the way it had been when they dated, but never referring to the past, just going on and on about people at work, her two dogs, shopping for children's clothes, working out in the company gym. Roger sensed an evasion in all she was saying, filling space to avoid confronting her real reason for being there. Once again, he felt a desperation about her, a need much more complex than he had realized as a teenager. He wished he could touch her face, comfort her.

He tried to change the subject, asking about people from their town. But Lauren knew nothing, had lost touch with almost everyone.

He looked at the clock over the bar and realized he didn't have more to say, nothing that was safe. "I'd better be getting home."

"Walk me to my room," she said. "It's just around the corner from the elevator to the garage."

Roger followed behind her, Lauren rattling on about how great it was to see him, how happy she was that he was happy, though he had never told her that.

He took the room card from her hand and unlocked the

door, pushing it open for her. She stood in the doorway. "Well." She reached out the same way she had for the formal hug when they had met earlier in the evening. He moved toward her but just touched her sleeve, convinced that if he held her she would have fallen into his arms, the two them plunging toward the bed, wild for each other.

Often, in the years that followed, Roger relived those few hours, along with the scenes of adolescent desire, trying to reconcile the two Laurens, as if hoping to see beyond the blur of a double exposure. The more he searched his memory, the more certain he was that the evening had all gone wrong, that he had missed obvious clues, that Lauren had summoned him for something he failed to provide. It wasn't just sex, perhaps not sex at all, though that would have been a fulfillment, at least for him. But she wanted more, something he was unable to understand.

Libby sent him an email message, not like the five a day she turned out for a group list, filled with exclamation points, about people who were coming to the reunion, attached photos, links to web sites, details of families and career. Usually Roger just skimmed them; he didn't really care. This was addressed to him alone, titled GOOD NEWS!!!!, all in capitals.

Libby was one of those people who had to describe each step of a process before she got to the main point. Roger had done so well in finding others that she thought he deserved help with Lauren. The exciting news, Libby reported, was that she had discovered a Simon Duryea in Philadelphia. Not a common name. It must be Lauren's brother. She gave Roger an email address. Surely, Simon would know. "Success ahead!!!" Libby was pushing to achieve one hundred percent identification of class addresses. Wouldn't it be wonderful if everyone came? "Imagine!" she wrote. "Thirty years!!!"

Roger tried to picture Simon and remembered that as much

time as he had spent with Lauren in those months, he rarely saw her brother, a scrawny twelve-year-old with knobby elbows, big feet, and thick, oversized glasses. The boy would come thumping down the stairs to rush into the kitchen to paw through a cutlery drawer and then run back up to his room with a knife or a scissors, oblivious of his father's fierce glare of disapproval, of his sister, and, certainly, of his sister's date.

One time Roger had asked Lauren about her brother, how it was to be an older sister, curious to understand how his own sister might have felt about him. "He's a nasty little thing," Lauren had said, laughing in such a way that Roger couldn't tell whether she were serious.

"Does he annoy you?"

"Hardly. He acts as if I don't exist."

"I'd find that impossible," Roger had said and pulled her into a kiss that left the two of them trembling.

Roger's vague memory of the boy came from the few times he had visited Lauren's home. Something about her family had made Roger uneasy, the strange silence, her father always in a suit, even on weekends, a tall lean man with a narrow mustache; her mother in a starched apron arranging flowers. That's the only thing he ever saw her do, yet the house was pristine, the wood polished, the metal gleaming. Simon was always locked in his room building intricate models, a dizzying odor of airplane cement penetrating the thick floral scents. When she was away from home, laughing, chattering on, the words spilling from her, Lauren, unlike the others in the family, wasn't eerily quiet, . But in her home, her presence seemed vague. Or maybe it had been him, afraid to stand near anyone, never close enough to touch Lauren, as if just touching would be a defilement in those rooms.

Roger sat at his keyboard for an hour before writing Simon, unsure how to word the message, whether to mention that he and Lauren used to date, that he had visited their house, that Simon might remember him. Should he be friendly, the way one is when getting in touch with an old acquaintance? If this first note were formal and businesslike, how would he explain himself if Simon responded with veiled annoyance at his impersonality? And what did it matter? All he wanted was information about Lauren.

When the Simon Duryea he had emailed did not respond in a week, Roger thought he had the wrong man, another person who was not even going to bother acknowledging a non-existent sister. Still, he thought he might resend. Email messages do get lost or deleted by mistake. Perhaps this Simon, fearing viruses, screened for anyone not on his secure list.

But the same afternoon Roger decided to try again once he read his inbox messages, there was one from "duryeas." Roger delayed opening it, checking the others first, those from people in his company, then deleting spam that offered low-interest loans or cut-rate Viagra.

He had to go over Simon's words several times before they sank in, run together in one long paragraph, all lower case. Simon recalled someone named Roger, no more: *lauren and i lost touch years and years ago. and she moved several times though I have no idea where she lives now. i don't remember her married name. I don't know if she ever had children. she might have gotten divorced. not long ago—i don't remember how—i heard a rumor that she was very ill, may even be housebound, bedridden. but i have no information about her condition. i know nothing that would help you find her.*

For the rest of the afternoon Roger sat with clenched fists, furious, wishing he could punch Simon's face. How could a man ignore his only sister, not care about reports of a serious illness? That night he lay awake, Evelyn curled on the mattress, facing the wall with the fluted breathing of her sleep, he imagining Lauren tight against him, so real he could taste her hair.

The next evening, Libby called, frantically curious. Roger could imagine her bouncing up and down in a chair. Tell me! Tell me! She groaned when he explained that Simon knew so little. Her disappointment, he knew, wasn't for Lauren but for a gap in her quest of locating all the lost ones. At that moment he decided he would do everything he could to find Lauren but tell Libby nothing.

"What was that about?" Evelyn asked.

"Nothing. Nobody who matters."

He sent a short note to Simon, pretending to thank him and asking if he could think of anyone who might know more. Simon returned the email with just the word "*no*" over Roger's original message. "What about old neighbors of your parents?" Roger responded and received in return, "*they're probably all dead too. people die.*"

"Not Lauren," Roger shot back. "Not so young."

He waited several days, checking the first thing when he turned on his office computer, even getting up in the middle of the night at home. It was there he discovered that Simon had written to him at 2 a.m. "*i don't care if lauren is alive or dead.*"

I DO. Roger pounded the keys, furious.

With a slam of his hand, Roger deleted Simon's message. He sat staring at the blank screen.

Roger walked to the men's room and splashed water into his eyes, staring at his face in the mirror and trying to imagine Simon standing beside him, grotesquely thin, one of his father's old suits hanging loose on his narrow frame, a tie tight on his throat, his hair wild in wispy strands, his flesh pale, thick, pink glasses halfway down his nose, the eyes crazed.

A scene took shape in his memory, his car parked in the street outside Lauren's house, his fingers inside her blouse rubbing her breast, her mouth against his ear emitting sounds of pleasure. Something made him open his eyes, look out through the soft strands of her hair. There at a bedroom window stood Simon, his glasses reflecting circles of moonlight. He had formed his hand into a pistol, aimed down at them, and squeezed. Roger was sure it had happened, that he had actually seen it, but never said a word to Lauren.

Roger wouldn't imagine Lauren seriously ill. He could only think of her as healthy, still lovely. He wondered if she really ever had a career, children, a husband named Vic, but knew it didn't matter. Her life had nothing to do with his.

Of course, he wouldn't attend the reunion. He would tell Libby it was Evelyn. They would be staying home because his wife didn't like crowds

The Way It Isn't

Alone on the screened porch, gazing up at the barren mountains that surrounded the lake, Carter had no idea why he was there, the real reason Valerie had invited Lydia and him to spend the weekend. They had been at this cabin two years ago, before Valerie left Les, before he and Lydia had their separation, before he and Valerie had their fling as lovers. Now he was Valerie's guest, though he was newly reunited with his wife, the two of them trying to reclaim their marriage, tentative, negotiating a contract.

Lydia had accepted immediately when Valerie called with the invitation, looking forward to the days in the woods and the chance to see Valerie again after so long; the last time they had gone to dinner with her and Les. "You don't see her any more now that's she taken a new job," she had told Carter. He had nodded his head, unable to think of a way to get out of it, not sure he wanted to.

Now Valerie was with Douglas, a man Carter couldn't make himself like. He saw why Valerie was attracted to him—tall, athletic, thick graying curls, but with stooped shoulders and an irritating metallic laugh. Mainly, he suspected, she could manipulate Douglas, just as she did most of the men who hovered around her, seeming eager for their advice, pretending helplessness. He had told her that once, in bed in a strange motel, legs intertwined in a lovemaking lull. "You're so wrong," she had pleaded, but he could sense annoyance, even though she had urged him to reveal all his thoughts, to hold back nothing. She had promised to be just as honest. When it was over, as loudly as she had screamed his name in anonymous rooms, as much as she had murmured words of love, he came to understand that for her it was only an affair. But she hadn't revealed *that* secret, and he hadn't admitted he knew.

The others were still sleeping. Carter had lain awake till he heard bird songs and threw on sweats to sip coffee and watch the birds swoop across the sunrise. He tried to convince himself how relaxing this all was, but, as still as he sat, couldn't stop churning.

In the middle of the night, stepping out from the second-floor bathroom, he had met Valerie in the hallway wearing only a pajama top. She just nodded with a thin smile as they maneuvered past each other, their arms brushing. He felt the heat of her, saw erect nipples pressing the cloth. Me or Douglas, he almost asked, the way he would have when they could say anything to each other. But all he did was mutter "Sorry," not sure she heard him.

Lydia came out to the porch before the others and pecked his cheek. "I didn't know what happened to you."

"Couldn't sleep. But you looked deep into it."

"It's this mountain air. Thanks for making coffee."

Carter shrugged. "I wanted some too."

Lydia pulled a chair next to his and leaned close to whisper. "It feels a bit odd being here. I mean, Valerie not with Les. Everything else feels so familiar."

"I don't miss Les."

"That's not what I meant." She gestured toward the cabin with a twist of her head. "What do you think of him?"

"Too soon to know."

"He seems to be trying very hard. Maybe it's because he knows we knew Les."

"That could be it." Carter wondered what else Douglas knew, unsure how he would react to a confrontation.

Lydia had her hand on Carter's arm when the door slammed back and Valerie and Douglas stepped onto the porch. "Hey, cut that out, you two." Douglas gave one of his laughs. Carter looked to Valerie for a reaction, but she was staring at the water.

"It's going to be a very pretty day," Lydia said.

"That's why Doug and I made our plan." Valerie turned back to the others. She was wearing shorts, her taut legs deeply tanned.

"What plan?" Carter didn't like the sound of it.

"It's been a while since Valerie and I have had a chance for a long talk," Lydia said. "We're going to treat ourselves to a picnic, and you and Doug will have a male-bonding day."

"How so?"

"A hike in the mountains, buddy." Douglas laughed and touched Carter's shoulder. "We'll climb high and look down at the world."

"I'm out of shape." Carter protested, upset that Valerie had conspired behind his back, suspecting something. He didn't want Lydia alone with her, but Lydia was smiling and nodding, and he didn't know how to stop them.

"Hey, I'll take it easy on you." Douglas winked at the women. "It's just a stroll, not a competition."

Douglas rubbed his palm over the mouth of a wine bottle and offered it. Carter shook his head. Douglas pounded the cork down with his fist and slid the bottle back into his rucksack. "So you want a clear head for our trek." He gestured toward the steep pathway of sharp grey rocks that led up into the trees above them. It was spring, but all around on both sides of the valley the highest mountains gleamed with snow at their peaks, ice crusted deep in the crevices.

Carter shivered even though his jacket was buttoned to his throat. Douglas wore only a short-sleeved shirt loose above faded jeans cut off at the knees. His heavy boots, wrapped in bright red laces, were scuffed raw at heel and toe. Carter glanced down at his own Reeboks, new for the weekend and bright white.

"Would you like to lead the way? Set the pace?" Douglas said.

"No, this is your territory. I'll just follow along."

Douglas moved quickly and surely, Carter tentative, wedging his foot tight before he shifted his weight. The path took a broad circle of steep inclines and sharp drops.

Douglas stopped on a ledge twenty feet ahead and turned to grin at Carter's methodical steps. "Tell me if you get tired. No need to rush. We have all day."

"I'm fine. Don't let my pace hold you back."

"We're in this together, buddy."

"Except that you know what you're doing."

"Don't be too sure." He hesitated, and Carter saw him swallow. "So tell me about Les."

"What about him?"

"All I can get out of Valerie is that it wasn't a happy marriage."

"It certainly wasn't." Carter felt a satisfaction at knowing so much more. She had confided in him even before they were lovers, when they were just coworkers meeting for lunch several times a week, occasionally socializing as couples. One day Valerie said, I feel so comfortable with you, and surprised him by weeping. From that moment, their lunches became a litany of Les's misdeeds—his foul mouth, his abuse of their sons, the time he slapped her. Carter found himself covering her trembling hands with his, telling himself he was comforting a friend, a very good friend, but each morning awaiting the opportunity to touch her. "They were much too young when they married," he told Douglas. "Incompatible."

"I get the sense that he was a major asshole."

"That too."

Douglas stepped back on the path and led Carter though a cluster of pines. A space in the trees offered a glimpse of the lake below, the cabins grouped at the far end. But Carter couldn't tell which was Valerie's. He tried to find a clearing where Lydia and Valerie could be having their picnic, wondering what he would say to Lydia if she confronted him with Valerie's confession, what that would do to their reconciliation.

Distracted, he slipped on a frozen patch, almost fell backwards, glad Douglas hadn't noticed. When he looked around, he saw loose boulders, deep plunges, dangers everywhere. For the first time he realized how far he could fall. But he wouldn't turn back, wouldn't spend the rest of the weekend with Douglas mocking his fear.

"Trouble ahead," Douglas called to him. They were stepping through a thin sheet of water that flowed over a bed of stones. Ten yards beyond, the stream rushed through jagged rocks. Douglas bounded across, hardly pausing as he moved from one surface to the other. Carter stood fixed on a boulder in the middle, the current swirling on both sides of him. If he slipped, he would plunge in icy water to his waist. He wasn't sure which direction to take, which rock was in his stride, which offered a firm footing.

Douglas looked back. "Be careful."

Carter brought both feet together and leaped to the bank, gripping a tree branch when he started to lose his balance. Douglas seized his wrist and pulled him up beside him. Carter wanted to twist away but feared falling.

The steep path narrowed and became slick with sodden leaves. Both men had to grip dank roots to drag themselves forward. Carter felt a film of perspiration under his shirt and unbuttoned his jacket. His Reeboks were caked with mud.

They came to a narrow, wooden bridge, three logs lashed together with vines, the spaces between them packed with dirt and clumps of weeds. The width of a man, the bridge offered no railings, nothing to hold onto. The ravine below was a deep drop, hundreds of feet onto dark points of stone.

"One at a time," Douglas cautioned before he stepped to the middle and waited until the logs stopped swaying. He moved off the bridge and stomped his boots on the path.

Carter paused at the edge, looked down, then rushed across the bridge, almost in a run. On the other side, he clung to a tree and felt his heart pounding. "You call this a stroll?"

"This is all new to me. Not what I expected at all." Douglas wasn't laughing.

Carter had a vision of the man tumbling off the bridge, plunging with a shriek that quivered the trees. When he told Valerie, she would collapse into his arms.

Douglas sat on a stump. "Time for a break."

Carter slid down against the tree and folded his legs, kneading a cramp in his calf. With his other hand he gouged a twig into the damp earth, pressing until it snapped.

"So what was the problem with you and Lydia?" Douglas said. "If you don't mind my asking."

Carter minded but wouldn't admit it. "The usual stuff." He remembered his silences at the dinner table, riding in the car, watching TV, unable to stop thinking of Valerie, the fantasy of her yielding to his embrace, afraid that if he spoke he would reveal it all. He hadn't encouraged Valerie to leave Les but did nothing to change her mind, wanting her free even though he wasn't. And when she was, Lydia was the one who asked him to go, telling him she couldn't live with a man who ignored her. Moments after he carried suitcases into a motel, he called Valerie to tell her. She met him that evening, the two of them sitting across a table in the dark corner of a tavern, both weeping, she gripping his hands this time. In a week they were lovers.

"How's it going now?" Douglas asked.

"Fine." When Valerie told him it was over, she had urged him to call Lydia. "She's the one for you, not me."

Douglas shook his head. "I'd be crazy to try to reconcile with my ex. I was crazy to marry her in the first place."

"It's not like that with us," Carter said. He began walking, unwilling to continue the conversation, Douglas scrambling behind him.

A thick sheet of grey ice covered the path ahead, slanting down over a lip of earth like a chute to the valley of tall spruces far below.

"Always prepared." Douglas reached behind into his rucksack and pulled out a pair of steel cleats that he clamped to his boots. He crossed the ice sheet as if dancing, lifting his bulk in ballet leaps and landing with loud crunching. "I'll throw you the cleats."

Was this Valerie's purpose, his humiliation by her new lover? Carter shook his head. "Never mind." He looked about him and snapped off two branches from a tree that overhung the path, trimming twigs until each branch was shaped like a claw. Then he got down on hands and knees and plunged the branches into the crust, one after the other. When he reached the other side, he stood and tossed the branches down into the valley. Douglas gave him a strange look.

Carter looked upward. "Where the hell are we?"

Beyond them, the path disappeared at a wall of rock ten feet high. Douglas shook his head. He went first, digging and cramming his toes into crevices to pull himself up. Carter followed, imitating him. The dark stone was very cold, coated with lichen that gave off a rank vegetable smell. Carter gasped open-mouthed, a burning in his back he knew would take months to heal. He moved up six inches at a time, his hands scratched and numb, eyes fixed on the soles of Douglas's boots, constantly afraid he would lose his grip and slide downward.

When he reached the top, he pitched forward and pressed his face into the earth. Douglas slumped against a tree. Carter dragged himself next to Douglas, exhausted, pain in his arms, his legs, the small of his back.

"We made it," Carter said. "But for what?"

"I have no idea." Douglas took a long gulp from the wine bottle.

Carter picked up a rock, shifting it from hand to hand, kneading it with his fingers. He stared down into the valley.

"What about Valerie?" Douglas said.

"How do you mean?"

"She tells me you two are very close."

"I guess we are."

Streaks of dirt ran down the sweat on Douglas's face. He tried to wipe it away but ended up with smears on his cheeks and forehead. "I asked her if there had ever been sex."

Carter squeezed the rock's sharp edges into his palm. "And what did she say?"

"That it isn't that way with you two."

Carter flung the rock, watching it tumble down through the brush and then disappear.

"I suppose it isn't."

He pulled himself up and waved a greeting toward the gleam of the lake far below, imagining Valerie looking up and seeing nothing more than a shadow on the rock face.

Host

When Luce met the Americans at the Marseille airport, feeling foolish to be holding up a sign with his name, he could see they were surprised to hear him speak in flat Midwestern tones, even when he shifted to French for the baggage clerks, fluent but unable to nasalize.

"We expected a native host," one of the women said, her hair close-cropped and dark even though she was as old as the others.

"I am," he told them. "In a way. I live here. As far as I know, it will always be where I live."

He expected a barrage of questions, accusations of disloyalty to the States. But one man said, "Lucky you. All this sunshine." And that was it.

Luce drove them in a rented van, six elderly couples, the first group of visitors he would host in the village, the start of his new occupation. It struck him that they were all in remarkable condition for their ages and then understood anybody who could afford this trip probably would be. He loaded their luggage into a low trailer hitched to the rear of the van and didn't stop the men from helping.

Luce watched them point at the landscape—the grey mountains in the distance, the absolute blue sky, the palms, the villages embedded into the rock face—each one animated, regarding the mundane details of his routine as scenic marvels. They had dozens of questions—about the weather, the food, the history—that he answered brusquely, without smiling. Though he was being paid to be cheerful, he doubted that it was in his nature.

At first he couldn't tell the American couples apart. He was too busy watching the road, constantly glimpsing the trailer in the side mirror as if he expected to lose it at the next bump in the road. Gradually, their voices started to take on distinctions. Eventually, he realized, he would come to know each one by name. At the end of the third week, when they were ready to go home, they would be as familiar as old acquaintances. That's the way it was with Americans—quickly met and quickly forgotten.

When he delivered them to the car rental agency on the highway outside the village, he saw one of the couples whispering under a tree, the wife glancing at him. It struck him that she was still a sexy woman, though decades too old for him, long grey hair swept over one eye, legs tanned, a suggestive thrust to her posture. The husband was trim in jeans and a baseball cap, swaggering like a teenager though he had to be close to seventy.

They were called, Luce learned by evening, Irene and Vern. Now he deciphered what she was whispering: "Should we tip him?"

For an instant, Luce was furious, ready to quit, drive off and leave them all stranded. Then he threw back his head and laughed, making the Americans look about them, eager to learn what was so funny.

His house in the village was a place Luce had chosen with Nicole, his French wife, wedged into a narrow street, four damp rooms with minimal light even when the shutters were open. Now she was gone with the children, back to her parents' vineyard at the base of a mountain, and he lived alone.

Luce's business had failed with the marriage, his third attempt to represent American companies in a territory that ranged from Avignon to Nice, this time farm equipment, spending hours drinking the local wines, discussing soils and seeds and weather, perfecting his agricultural vocabulary but selling little.

The French language he had started in college, encouraged by A's in the classroom, though in practice, when he first arrived in the country, he made Nicole giddy at his barbarisms. Every time he spoke to her, she would place a hand on his arm and shake her head, "Non, non, non." One day, thinking why not, he covered her hand with his and didn't let go. Then he had been young and promising, on a two-year appointment with an American bank in Paris, she a national employed in the same department. Because of Nicole he stayed in France when the assignment ended, quit the bank, married and moved south to the Midi. As often as he asked her twelve years later, she wouldn't explain if her resentment was the result of his botched ventures or his morose reactions, his furious demands that their monolingual children speak English.

When Nicole left, taking one whole Saturday to load the children's furniture and her personal belongings in her father's open truck, no one in the village mentioned the fact to Luce, though everyone had seen and knew he had. They had known him as part of a family for a decade, and now treated him as if he had always been alone. Madame Duvall, the old widow directly across the street, forever hanging her bird cages outside and taking them back in at the hint of clouds, gave him stews several days a week, each time claiming that she had made too much for herself. Some of the men requested his help on projects—plastering walls, laying new drain pipe, never offering money but compensating with gifts of wine and food, a rabbit or a chicken, a wedge of blue-veined cheese.

Then, by a fluke, Luce fell into a job. A thumping on his front door startled him from an afternoon doze, and he opened it to a man who was clearly American, crewcut, all in khaki, looking like a retired general. "I need somebody bilingual," the man said. "People at the market tell me that's you." It turned out the man, Charlie Poling, had been a NATO officer for years. Now, in civilian life, he was a would-be travel entrepreneur, finding Americans flats in the south of France for three-week holidays. The villages around Luce's were perfect places, away from the tourist crowds but teeming with art and history, a short drive from the sea. He needed a local representative to check out accommodations, meet planes at Marseille, arrange rental cars, and troubleshoot. Pay would be on a per capita basis, so much for each vacationer. Luce would have an incentive for keeping people happy. "Build relationships for the future," Charlie told him. "This could keep us both going for years to come."

Every American, man and woman, was twenty to thirty years older than Luce, flourishing in retirement, hair in thick grey waves. They moved quickly, the women taut and smiling, the men broad-shouldered, flat-stomached, bounding on the mountain paths, up steep stone stairways.

From Charlie Poling's explanation, Luce had expected to be a geriatric caretaker. But when he met the first group, he stared at himself in the bedroom mirror, lifting his shirt, turning sideways, ashamed of his bloated middle. People had been feeding him too well with rich sauces, and he exercised too little.

The Americans were obsessed with fat and cholesterol, asking him more questions about diet than any other topic. Didn't any of the restaurants have healthy menus? They looked forward to excess now and then but weren't willing to clog their arteries for the sake of a small pleasure.

Luce made jokes about them to the villagers, waiting until the Americans were off on jaunts, not sure how many of them understood the language. "They dread delight." That was his refrain each time he mimicked their concerns, holding out a croissant at arm's length. "Horreur!" He would throw up his hands and let his eyes roll back. His neighbors responded with much laughter.

In the tavern, at Luce's lead, the men would imitate the Americans' movements, flip through imaginary guidebooks, peer down at a page and then point into the distance, shaking each other's shoulders in feigned excitement. They strode rapidly from one side of the room to the other, pretended to wolf down food, and rush out the door.

"But they are rich," François said one day, a large man with a shaggy black mustache who owned the garage but spent most of his time fishing on the river that curved through the village.

"Perhaps their money gives them energy," Jean-Paul suggested. He was their butcher, always carrying a small white poodle in a straw basket. Now it slept on the stool beside him.

"If Luce had stayed in America, he would be a rich man too." François broke into a wide grin and winked at Luce.

"Living in a huge house with a swimming pool," Patrice added from behind the bar, filling their glasses from a cask of red wine. "Driving a Cadillac. No, two."

"Eating only safe food and jogging twenty kilometers a day." Jean-Paul was grinning too, the men making a game of imagining Luce's American fortune.

Luce made himself smile back, as if he were amused. "But think. I would have missed so many refreshing times with such good friends." He lifted his glass and held it out to the sunlight. "And the best wine in the world."

"Which you have in the family." Jean-Paul tried to swallow his words as soon as he spoke. The other men looked down at the bar top.

Luce broke the silence. "Theirs was sour. I have a wider choice now." But he realized saying that was a mistake. It would have been better to ridicule the Americans again.

Irene and Vern were all over. Luce ran into them in the village almost every day, jogging down the main street in matching blue outfits before the shops opened, patronizing the boulangerie before the midday closing, buying one of Patrice's best wines in the evening. Yet they ranged for miles in their adventures, reciting itineraries for Luce as if he would be pleased to know. They had explored the Roman arenas at Nîmes and Arles, the theater in Orange, the caves at Chateauneuf du Pape, Cezanne's atelier in Aix, van Gogh's sanitarium in St. Remy, the bulls of the Camargue, the beaches at Cannes.

"How do you find the time?" Luce asked, exhausted just to contemplate their days, watching the old men of the village crouched in their perpetual game of boules on a triangle of dirt behind the shops.

"It's the air here," Irene told him. "It energizes."

"We've barely begun." Vern jingled his car keys.

"How long have you two been married?" Luce surprised himself with the inquiry because he rarely asked personal questions.

They looked at each other as if to decide who would have the pleasure of answering. Vern gestured with his chin, and Irene said, "Forty-two years."

"Have you always been this way?" Luce said.

"What way?" Irene winked, and Vern hugged her.

Luce had loved Nicole, but he had trouble telling her. "Je t'aime" didn't seem right coming from him, not the way it sounded in French movies. Though she never did, he always expected her to laugh and correct his accent. And "I love you" seemed foreign, inappropriate in this place, with this woman. So, in the first years, he gave her caresses, seizing her for sudden kisses in the hope that he was expressing himself.

But over the years, when the children came and need led her to become a cashier in the village bank, the only work available despite her supervisory experience in Paris, he began to sense that such physical expression was an infringement. She was always so tired; the children were always about, watching everything their parents did. Even as toddlers they spoke their first words with such perfect accents that Luce couldn't believe they were his.

"Has this been a mistake?" Nicole came to ask him, more and more frequently.

"What?" he would say each time, as if he had no idea what she meant.

And should would repeat, as if in a ritual, "Leaving your country. Making your life here."

"I'm very happy," he would tell her, sure she was wondering how could someone who had such great promise as a young man be such a failure now.

Then she stopped asking, soon after announced that she was leaving, and two days later appeared with her father's rusted truck, the children helping her load, Luce standing rigid on the stones of the street, uncertain whether he should offer to help too.

Charlie Poling called at noon one day with an idea. Why didn't the villagers throw a party, a picnic, for their American visitors? Extend local hospitality and boost the economy.

Luce didn't like it. He almost told Charlie he didn't want to mix his life and his job, though he knew his real concern was that one of the villagers—Jean-Paul—would slip into the mockery he had initiated.

But François was enthusiastic when Luce started to grumble about the assignment. "It will be a great entertainment, my friend. We'll all be very amused."

"I thought people in the village resented the Americans," Luce said. "Walking around with their cameras and their maps while everybody else works."

"You've got it all wrong. We love the Americans. They stroll about with baguettes under their arms. They smile at us and say, 'Bonjour.' It's as if they've finally discovered life in their old age."

"Would you want them to stay?"

"Of course not. One permanent American is enough for any village." François wrapped Luce in his large arms and loomed over him, a head taller.

François and Patrice made the arrangements for the picnic with the Americans, calling it a fête, planning for hours, treating it like a sport. They waved off Luce's suggestions, sent him on errands. "You organize your countrymen," they told him. "Make sure they don't get lost on the way to the park."

Everyone gathered on the bank of the river just outside the village, where great trees shaded an expanse of rich grass and branches overhung a broad pool of water. Bright sun gleamed from the rippling surface, and flowering shrubs colored the fields of the opposite bank. The Americans exclaimed as they arrived on the path from the car park, overwhelmed by the setting. The villagers, all there in advance, nodded at each other, proud that this was their home. But Luce moved among them anxiously, rearranging canvas chairs, straightening the tableware, making introductions, waiting for the first disaster.

There was much handshaking, broad grins. Several villagers spoke a little English, and a few of the Americans' words of broken French, each amused at the other's efforts, as if their failures in communication were a comic performance. Everyone was making elaborate gestures, touching their chests, sweeping hands outward toward the horizon. Luce had no idea what they were trying to say.

François got them all seated, alternating Frenchmen and Americans at an assemblage of folding tables twenty feet long. "Hello down there," one of the Americans called to people at the other end, and everyone laughed. François sat between Irene and Vern, turning from one to the other, speaking the phrases he had rehearsed with Luce.

Patrice poured wine, a bottle of red in one hand, white in the other. There were five or six toasts. The mayor, the only person wearing a suit, made a speech that Luce felt compelled to translate, summarizing every hundred words in ten. "He welcomes you all on behalf of the village. He's very happy that we have so many new friends. He wishes you great enjoyment in his country."

Food was served, François up and about, helping Patrice and Jean-Paul and a group of the local women pass around platters heaped with paté and chops and pizza and salad. Old Madame Duvall carried a stack of baguettes in her apron, handing out one to every person at the table, overjoyed at their thanks. Despite the guests' inability to understand the locals, the gathering was raucous, much laughter, the same words shouted again and again as if in lessons. Jean-Paul's poodle ran among them, wagging its stub of a tail, yipping happily. Glasses were raised and touched. Patrice wiped his brow, lifted his eyes to the blue sky, and hurried back to the car park for another case. Luce sat at one end of the table, surprised when the others turned to toast him, as if all this had been his doing. He smiled back, touched his own glass to his lips, but did not drink.

It perplexed Luce that people who had mocked the Americans so much could suddenly behave as their friends. It had taken years before they allowed him to become part of the village even though Nicole had been a great favorite.

At the end of the meal, Jean-Paul carried in a huge cake that he had baked himself, thick with white icing and decorated with crude approximations of the French tricolor and the Stars and Stripes. People exclaimed. Luce heard Vern's loud, "Tres bien!" The mayor made the first slice, and Madame Duvall passed around wedges on paper plates. People ate with plastic forks, licking their fingers.

Then the village children appeared from behind the trees, the girls costumed in billowing dresses of the delicate local prints, the boys in dark trousers and ruffled shirts. A single musician banged a drum strapped to his middle and blew into a wooden pipe. The children danced, circling, clasping hands, converging and fanning out over and over again. The little ones stumbled to keep up, but the teenagers were graceful and synchronized. One tall girl, barefoot, hair loose to her waist, leaped into the center and twirled on her toes while the others spun rings about her. The Americans were on their feet, cheering, snapping photographs, Irene and Vern both clinging to François's shoulders, as if they were sharing something quite wonderful.

For all his years in the village, Luce had never seen these costumes or these dances. He wondered when they practiced, whether his own children had been among them without his ever knowing it.

When the dancing was over and the table cleared, the park quieted, people sprawled in their chairs, the villagers lighting pipes and cigarettes, the Americans not smoking, just leaning back and studying the trees.

Then Luce heard a splash of water. François was coiling a rope and pushing his flat-bottomed boat away from the bank. Irene was with him, sitting in the rear, running both hands through her rich grey hair. François stood and pushed his long pole at the river bottom. The boat rounded a bend and disappeared behind the trees.

Luce looked for Vern, curious to see the man's expression, and was surprised to find him approaching, reaching out to seize his hand in a solid grip. "Terrific party, Luce. The highlight of our vacation."

"Glad you like it," Luce muttered. "The villagers did all the work."

"I'm really pleased we came here. This is one of the greatest places in the world. But I don't have to tell you that."

"Actually," Luce said, "you've seen much more than I have. Just about everywhere I've gone since I moved here has involved some kind of work."

"But you're missing so much."

"I've seen almost nothing."

A crazy image flashed into Luce's imagination, François's boat sheltered under a sweeping branch, Irene seducing him, the two of them with jeans down to their ankles, the boat rocking.

"Then do yourself a favor." Vern squeezed his shoulder, a friendly gesture that gave him pain. "Live a little."

Luce looked out toward the river and watched François and Irene reappear on the river in the drifting boat, seated side by side, sharing a bottle of wine, laughing happily as they saluted him with their glasses.

He lifted his glass in return, then threw it in the river, the red wine streaking out and quickly dissipating. Vern gave him an odd look and touched his arm.

At the contact, Luce pulled away and leaped into the water, just stood there, submerged to the waist, his shoes stuck in the muddy bottom, the wine glass between them. Without looking up, from the silence, he could tell that everyone on the bank had stopped their conversations to watch him. He heaved forward with a loud splash and let himself sink into the chill current, inert, arms at his side, refusing to breathe.

Eyes closed, Luce felt men lift him out, knew from the voices that it was François, Patrice, Jean-Paul, and Vern. They set him on the grass, François miming the kiss of life, exaggerating his gestures, huffing and groaning, as if saving Luce were an elaborate joke, an entertainment staged for the occasion. Circled around him, all the others—French and Americans—united in laughter.

Dreaded

The moment Graham stepped into the room behind Ed Aquilla, he recognized the young woman. She was sprawled on the wooden floor, tripped backwards as if she had lost her footing, arms splayed above her head, one leg wrenched at the knee. "Oh my god, it's Dreaded!" Graham's words came out as a gasp that Ed didn't seem to hear. He was kneeling beside the body, his broad back straining against the blue policeman's uniform, his hands already in latex gloves.

"Her name is Deirdre," Graham said, this time loud, urgent information. "My daughter Holly roomed with her. But only a few months." He repeated the name. "Deirdre." The sound felt odd to him. With Holly, he had called her Dreaded, demanding that Holly move out at once, find another place, come back home. Get away from Dreaded.

Still silent, Ed touched one finger to the carotid artery. But it was clear that she was dead, the way the empty eyes gaped upward. Her body didn't seem injured—no wounds or blood or bruises. Yet Graham knew she had been killed. He had predicted it a year ago, shouting at Holly, "That girl is trouble! One night you'll open the door and find her murdered!" But he had imagined blood splatters, knife slashes, bullet holes, mutilation.

Graham backed toward the doorway, hands deep in his pockets, knowing he shouldn't touch anything in that room, afraid his few footsteps had been a mistake.

Next to the size of Ed Aquilla, the body looked like that of a child. There was nothing to her, scrawny legs protruding from pajama bottoms, brittle arms in a dirty tee shirt, the face gaunt, pale, scabbed. Drugs, disease, malnutrition. She barely came to Holly's shoulder. It had tortured Graham to see his daughter sharing space with Dreaded.

He considered calling Holly with the news. "See, see. I was right. Somebody killed her." Then he realized that might make Holly hate him.

Ed was the one to flip open a phone, telling someone to send an ambulance and the coroner. Then he spoke to Graham. "I'm sorry. I didn't expect we'd find this."

"I should know these things. What you have to face and how you manage it."

The two men had been sitting with coffee cups at the police station phone bank when the call came, a raw male voice saying he was sure something was wrong in an apartment, blurting an address, and hanging up. Graham was there because the town council made him liaison to the department, and he had taken to spending evenings in the building, telling people he did it because of his responsibility but knowing it was an excuse to fill time now that he and Maggie were living apart. She was still in the house, he in a condo he couldn't sell, his stuff stored in a stack of boxes.

Ed Aquilla and he had become friends, talking more about local real estate than police work. That was Graham's profession. Ed moonlighted as a painter on days off, and Graham had begun recommending him when he advised clients to spruce up their property.

When he heard the caller give the address, Graham knew the house, though he wouldn't have guessed the something wrong was Dreaded. It wasn't where she had shared an apartment with Holly. He had been one of a list of agents who tried to sell the place, a series of realtor signs posted on the front lawn. But he and the others knew it was futile, shared their pessimism at agents' gatherings. Dilapidated, yard overgrown, roof sagging, wedged between a gas station and a rundown machine shop. Who would want to live there? Who could see a profit in renting rooms to people desperate enough to have to?

"You probably shouldn't be here," Ed told him. "Anyway, there won't be room when all the others arrive."

Graham nodded. "I'll wait in the car."

Soon after he got into the front passenger's seat, he heard sirens, two more police cars swerving around the corner with flashing lights and siren blasts as if a crime were still in progress. People had complained at Council meetings. "All that noise just because somebody ran a stop sign." The cops in town were bored. He knew it. They would roar to a brush fire, congregate at the scene of a fender bender, men and a couple of women with college degrees whose main function was public service. Directing traffic, making a presence at school events, helping with flat tires. And now they had a murder.

Graham pictured them crowded around the body, gawking, trying to grasp that someone had killed a young woman in their town. Dreaded. A human being he had met a few times, didn't like, considered a threat to his daughter. He felt shame at his relief.

What if Holly had still been rooming with her? She might have been there when the killer arrived. A second victim. He couldn't shut out the image of Holly lying on that floor, her thick black hair tangled under her skull, her gray eyes vacant. He clutched his hands over his knees, awash in cold sweat. Then it struck him that Ed, the police, would want to question Holly about the months she had spent with Dreaded.

Holly didn't answer her cell phone. "Hi. Tell me something good." Loud music behind her greeting, heavy guitar chords, smashing drums. But Graham wouldn't leave a message, didn't want to inform her that way.

Maggie should know too. Holly lived with her mother in the home where she had spent almost her entire life. When he moved out, she moved back in. At the time he told himself he had sacrificed his marriage to get his daughter away from Dreaded. But he couldn't really believe that. It was all the shouting, the days and days of sullen silence that had driven Holly out of the house. He knew they should stop for the sake of their daughter. But they didn't, couldn't. One night they found her in the front hallway, duffle bags over both shoulders, suitcases in her hands. Maggie had tried to embrace her but couldn't get past the luggage. He had just called Holly's name and "Don't." But his daughter was out the door without a word, not even a goodbye. He and Maggie had stared at each other until he finally said, "She'll be back." Maggie let out a wail and ran upstairs. It turned out he had been right. Holly was back. He wasn't.

Graham parked on the street, unwilling to pull into the driveway. It felt strange to stand on the front porch and ring the chimes. Even though he had a key, he wouldn't use it. When no one answered, he looked at his watch. Just before ten. Maggie might have gone to bed, but not Holly. He rang again and this time heard footsteps on the stairs, sensed an eye peering at him though the peephole and guessed it was Maggie. He wondered if she would turn away, deny him. They hadn't spoken in several months beyond a few exchanges of voicemail. But she opened the door very slowly, as if ready to slam it shut. "Yes?" she said, the uncertain way she would respond to a salesman.

"I have to talk to Holly."

"Holly is out with friends."

"She's not answering her phone."

"They went to a movie."

"Then I'd better tell you."

She opened the door wide enough for him to enter but blocked the way to the living room. He'd have to stand in that small space.

Maggie was wrapped in a pink fleece robe, one he didn't remember, her hair rolled in curlers, her face washed of makeup. He didn't feel anger any more. Seeing her after so long didn't arouse any emotion. Not regret, not yearning, not sadness. Perhaps it was the news he bore, what it might mean for their daughter.

"Do you remember Deirdre?" He used the real name.

She nodded, eyes puzzled.

"I was at police headquarters when a call came in. I went with Ed Aquilla." Graham knew that these details didn't matter. Still he couldn't come out and say it.

"Yes? So?" He could tell she was beginning to get annoyed with him, all the times she had shouted, "Get to the point."

"Deirdre's been murdered."

Maggie's face fell. "Oh, that poor girl." She was weeping though she hadn't approved of the roommate any more than he had. He remembered her yelling at him: "Don't call her Dreaded."

They stood close enough for him to reach out and comfort her. A pat on the arm, a touch to her shoulder. But he did nothing. Perhaps Maggie's tears came for the same reason he had been shaken: It could have been Holly. Someone could have murdered Holly.

Graham clutched the doorknob. He had to get away from her grief. "Let Holly know what happened. And tell her she has to call me."

"Why?"

"The police will want to talk to her."

"What for? What did Holly do?"

"She lived with the woman. She might have information."

"It was you. She never would have moved in with that person if it hadn't been for you."

Graham stomped down the path to his car, sat and took deep breaths before he could drive off.

He expected Holly to call early in the morning, but she didn't. The few calls he received were from clients about open houses and pending contracts. Ed phoned to ask if he were ok and said he had to go as soon as Graham told him he was. He waited until he knew Holly was at work and speed-dialed her. She was number 2, right after 1 for emergencies.

Caller ID must have identified him. She said hello, her voice distant. He missed the enthusiasm of her recorded message.

"Did your mother tell you?" he asked.

"Yes, she told me." Flat, no emotion.

"Did she explain that you and I have to talk?"

"We're very busy today. Deadlines."

"This can't wait. Meet me for lunch."

"I was going to skip lunch to get work done."

"You have to see me." It was a command.

The pause lasted so long he thought she had hung up. Then, "All right."

In the restaurant Graham wondered if she would show, glancing down at his watch again and again past the time they were supposed to meet. He had chosen a steakhouse on the highway, too fancy for a lunch but one he knew would be almost empty at midday, offering privacy. Two men at the bar were familiar; but he just nodded when the hostess led him past them. He rearranged his silverware, knotted an edge of tablecloth in his lap.

When Holly appeared in the entranceway, he covered the watch with his hand so he wouldn't look down, determined not to mention her lateness. Fortunately, she was wearing slacks, not a skirt and not the shorts she insisted on wearing from early spring late into the fall. His daughter had a lovely face, much more attractive than either of her parents. He had spent fruitless hours during her adolescence trying to determine what features of his and Maggie's had combined in Holly. But her legs were wrong, out of proportion, short and thick. Did she know how unflattering the shorts were? Was wearing them an act of defiance, flaunting a defect? Of course, he couldn't ask and couldn't stop wondering what other defects he didn't know about. Maggie was always telling her how pretty she was, he nodding in agreement. Smiles animated her face. She wasn't smiling now.

He considered standing to pull back her chair and decided that would be too obvious. Even before she sat, she said, "I told you it wasn't a good day. They weren't happy I went out."

"This is important."

She nodded, mouth fixed.

He pressed the question. "Are you upset?"

Holly shrugged, flipped her dark hair back over her shoulder.

"She was just somebody I knew."

"You lived with her. Six months"

"I've lived with you and mother more than twenty years."

Graham met her eyes, a signal to explain. She stared back, unblinking.

"The police are going to want to talk with you."

Holly closed one fist around a fork, the other around a knife, pointed them straight up. "That makes sense. They want to know if I have any idea about who killed her."

He hadn't let himself consider that possibility, unwilling to believe Holly had known the same people as Dreaded. "How could you?"

"I'll save any suspicions I have for your police."

He reached out and covered her hand with his, pressed it down to the tabletop. "You know I'm the Council's liaison with the police."

She pulled her hand free. "Why did you have to get on the Council anyway? People didn't vote for you."

"I didn't run. They asked me to fill out a term when Bob McMillan got transferred to Oregon. I thought it would help me stay busy once I was on my own."

"You should have taken up woodworking."

"Holly, please tell me. What do you know?"

She pulled her cell phone from her purse and checked the time. "I have to get back. They'll fire me." Graham could see her shifting on the padded chair and sensed she was about to stand up.

"What about eating?"

"I suppose I'll have to go hungry. There are worse things."

Halfway to the exit, Holly turned and spoke to him, so loud the men at the bar stopped their conversation. "I knew this would happen to her."

In his office Graham tried to do paperwork, spread forms across his desktop and sat over them with a pencil. After an hour, he slashed a long mark across one sheet and told his secretary he was going out. Council work.

At police headquarters, he couldn't find Ed Aquilla. The woman at the desk told him he was with the coroner. Graham said he would wait and poured coffee in the break room, stirring in cream, though he usually took it black. When he realized what he had done, he dumped the cup into the sink.

He rehearsed in his thoughts what he might say to Ed: Can we speak off the record? Holly knows something she won't tell me, only to the police. But maybe she didn't. Maybe her claim of suspicions was merely a way of upsetting him. Maybe she knew nothing at all. But maybe something she told Ed would just cause trouble for her. For him. For all of them.

Ed came into the room and sat at the table. "I heard you were here."

"What did the coroner say?"

"I should have looked more closely. Somebody pinched her windpipe. Suffocated her. She was such a frail thing. She couldn't fight back."

"Would it have mattered if you noticed?"

"No. But I'm supposed to be observant."

"Did they find drugs?"

"Sure. But that's not what killed her."

Graham shook hands with the man, something he never did when they parted, deciding not to ask when he planned to talk to Holly.

He microwaved a Lean Cuisine for dinner and drank water, pulling the pitcher from behind the wine bottles in his refrigerator. The TV news played in the other room, then switched to what must have been a comedy, fake laughter sounding in the background. He didn't pay attention, just waited for the time to pass until it was night.

Parked outside his old house, Graham had no idea if Holly were home, uncertain what he would reveal to Maggie if she weren't. But he knew he had to tell her mother about his concern.

This time Maggie opened the door wide as if she wanted him

to come inside. "Did she say anything to you?" he whispered. She shook her head. He asked her to bring Holly down.

The first thing he saw on the stairway was her thick legs in faded denim shorts, ragged edges high up her thighs. She clumped clogs down on each step as she descended. "I was going out."

"It's chilly tonight," he told her.

"I don't get cold."

"I'm worried about you."

"Isn't it a bit late for that?"

"I'm not talking about the temperature." He saw Maggie hovering at the edge of the room, read her familiar expression of concern and felt sorry for her. He felt sorry for all of them, the remains of a family stiff on a grey carpet.

His intention was to tell Holly what Ed Aquilla had reported but instead asked, "Why did you move in with someone like her?"

"Dreaded?" The way she sneered the name mocked him. "You probably think it was your fault. The two of you being horrible to one another. All those shouts and glares and slammed doors. Dad, don't flatter yourself. You're not that important."

"But you came back as soon as I left."

"Because I was terrified." An edge of fear distorted her face. Maggie stepped toward her.

"Of what? Of her?"

"I moved in with Deirdre because I wanted to be with her. We shared interests."

"Drugs?"

"That and other things."

Maggie shook her head. "It couldn't be. I never saw any signs."

"Mother, you wouldn't know a sign if it bit you. I've had the benefits of living with the two of you. I'm very good at deception."

"So what changed?" Graham asked, surprised by how calm he was being.

"There were people I hadn't known about, hadn't anticipated."

"The people who killed her?"

She folded her arms across her chest. "Probably. No, certainly."

He wouldn't ask what their motive could have been, didn't want to know. "Will you tell that to the police?"

"If I did, those people would kill me too."

Maggie clung to her daughter's shoulders, trying to embrace her, but Holly resisted. "So what do you want me to do, Daddy? Mr. Police Liaison?"

It wasn't even a decision. "I'll tell Ed Aquilla I spoke with you. That you barely knew her or anything about her life. All you did was see an ad for a roommate. But he'll have to interview you himself."

"And you want me to repeat your lie."

"Yes. That's what I want."

Sobbing, Maggie wrapped her arms around Holly. Holly was sobbing too, mother and daughter huddled in tears. Graham couldn't look at them. He turned and walked out of the house, his hand trembling on the doorknob as he pulled it shut.

Night Sounds

Hot, jetlagged, drained from a meeting that had lasted through his first afternoon in Brussels, Lewis flopped onto the soft bed just after nine. Near midnight, sleepless, suffocated by humidity, he threw off the sheet and swung open the window for air. At once the room echoed with night sounds from the narrow street—car mufflers, shouted conversations, rattling glass, radios, trucks rumbling over the cobblestones, barking dogs, motor scooters, babies' cries. But he was desperate for the slightest breeze.

Later, wide awake, he sat up, wiped sweat from his face with the sheet, and slumped back again, bunching the damp pillow under his arm, frantic for comfort. He squinted at the clock radio, the digits blurred without his glasses. 2 a.m. Hours of a sweltering night still to endure.

Lewis hadn't expected Brussels to be so hot, his garment bag stuffed with wool suits and sweaters for the weeks ahead. But the moment he stepped outside the air terminal that morning, a sultry blast had engulfed him. The taxi driver said it had been like a furnace all week, no end in sight.

He lay with burning eyes, identifying each sound like solving pieces of a puzzle. But they didn't make any sense. It was as if the quiet street of the afternoon, rue Bordiau, became a Babel of noises when darkness fell. The problem was all acoustics, he told himself, each sound magnified unnaturally in the empty night.

Lewis would be here for a month, sent by his company to negotiate with officials of the European Union, living in a furnished apartment on the second floor of a three-story building just a short walk from the complex of EU offices. The rental agent had been waiting with a key when his taxi arrived, a small woman with large round glasses. She demonstrated how to secure the double bolts in the thick wood entrance door but told him not to worry—the neighborhood was peaceful; then she shook his hand and drove off in a BMW, leaving him bewildered. He only had time to unpack his bags and shower before rushing to his meeting.

When he had turned the corner on rue Archimede and saw the Complexe Berlaymont, he froze to stare, stunned by the sweeping grey arcs of the abandoned building. The EU representatives he had met in the States had explained in advance: the organization's headquarters was vacant because of asbestos contamination; it would take years to make it safe for use. As the building loomed above him in the haze, he had shuddered at the sensation of all those hollow corridors, deserted offices. He imagined being trapped in the huge, forsaken structure, fleeing dangers, racing through a maze of hallways into a tangle of dead ends.

Wide awake now, sitting up with his head propped against the wall, Lewis heard a woman's footsteps approaching from a block away, the clipped strikings of high heels, getting louder as she approached, reaching a peak just below his window, then fading as she moved past. The Doppler effect, he thought, and wondered who she was, what she was doing out so late. Streetwalker. The idea struck him, absolutely literally, but not on rue Bordiau, not in such a residential neighborhood far from the city's center.

Usually, travel to new cities made him dream of sex, ardent encounters with beautiful strangers, absolute physical pleasure. But it was too hot even for that fantasy. Lewis missed his wife, imagined her pressed against him as they slept in an air-conditioned bedroom, children peaceful across the hall. This flat on rue Bordiau had no cooling, not even a fan, because Brussels was supposed to be a temperate city. But the world's climate was changing. Nothing was as it was supposed to be.

Dozing when the alarm rang, Lewis jumped out of bed with his skin slick and eyes stinging. He stumbled into the bathroom, then remembered the toilet was in a separate cubicle. But he splashed his face with cold water first, toweled himself dry.

The coffeemaker was gurgling as he came out of the shower, and the grains from the gold foil packet left on the counter tasted like strong expresso. Lewis shook his head at the bitterness but poured another cup. The only food in the apartment was a bagette and a stick of butter. He tore the bread in half and realized how hungry he was. As he chewed, he clicked on the TV and found nothing but a cartoon in French, and CNN—familiar reporters' faces narrating scenes of war and famine. Human beings lay dying in the mud, their emaciated arms reaching out at nothing. He blanked the screen with the remote and bit through the crust.

The morning was already hot when Lewis stepped onto the street at 8 a.m., checking his jacket for the key, pulling the building door closed, rattling it to make sure the lock had caught.

A few people were walking ahead, carrying briefcases or canvas bags. But the street was so quiet. No steps rang out, and even the vans on the next block seemed muffled, the noise of the night dispersed by daylight.

His building was the most elegant in the neighborhood, red brick with wrought iron balconies, the white trim of the windows freshly painted. All the other buildings along the street had balconies too, some thick with potted flowers. But most needed refurbishing, a cleaning of their surfaces, neat curtains in the windows, a filling in of cracks and gouges. Lewis recognized it as an area in transition, valuable because it was so close to the offices of the European future.

When he noticed the shop on the next corner, its narrow windows stacked with cans and boxes, crates of fruits and vegetables tiered on the sidewalk outside, it struck him that he should shop for food. The sign over the door said Pakistani Grocery, and the owner, a small, stooped man with a pencil mustache, eyed him suspiciously as he scanned the shelves in confusion, still hungry but with no idea of what he should buy. He sought out familiar brands and loaded his arms with cereal boxes, canned meats and vegetables, a carton of milk. When he dumped it all on the wooden counter, the grocer seemed annoyed, grim-faced as he tabulated each item on a manual cash register, grudgingly tearing off a plastic bag for Lewis to carry his purchases.

"Have a nice day," Lewis said as he left to return to his apartment, wondering if he had time to take another shower but realizing that would be useless in this weather.

Halfway to his building he passed an elderly Arab woman squatting in a doorway and rolling a large, multicolored ball across the sidewalk to a child standing at the curb. The woman wore layers of black down to her ankles, a white scarf covering her hair and knotted under her chin. Deep lines radiated from her mouth, sagged under her glistening dark eyes. The child, a little girl, couldn't have been more than two, with a head of black curls, probably a granddaughter. In a flowered dress and pink sandals, she flopped on the ball and tumbled into the gutter, struggling to pick it up. From her face, she took the activity very seriously, and the grandmother did not smile.

"*Bon jour*," Lewis said to her, but it was as if he had not spoken.

Against the wall of the building just past the woman's door were propped the pieces of an old bed frame—a wooden headboard, slats, metal railings, a naked box spring. The debris annoyed him; he expected order in European cities.

All day during his meetings, the EU representatives polite, their English impeccable, Lewis could not keep from staring out the window across Robert Schuman Circle to the rows of blank windows in the Complexe Berlaymont. If these people had blundered so badly with their headquarters building, he wondered, what other mistakes were they making? What else didn't they know? He wanted so much for everything to make sense.

Returning to the apartment at the end of the day, Lewis walked through Square Marguerite, following the neat row of trimmed trees spaced along the gravel path, studying the design of the handsome buildings across the park. Here was the Europe he had hoped to find. At that hour, people were out with their dogs, small delicate creatures walking briskly on narrow leashes.

He ate in a restaurant that evening, Italian food in a garden behind a formal dining room in a stone building on the rue Archimede. Even though it was past eight, Lewis sat alone at a metal table as the only customer, the tuxedoed waiters clustered around the door, sullen with inactivity until a group arrived, obviously longtime customers, exuberant in their greetings, served wine as soon as they took their chairs, toasting with great enthusiasm.

Lewis looked at his watch and wondered what he would do for a month of evenings. The day still had not cooled. Even though the sun was setting, everything felt damp, even the napkin on his lap. For his wife, back home, it was early afternoon, and he had already called her a few hours before from his cell phone after the meetings. All he had to tell her was how hot it was in Brussels and that he missed her. She missed him too. Their children were playing with friends. He'd talk to them another time, he said, and felt an ache of absence.

Back in the apartment he tried to read but ending up turning on the TV, sitting in shorts and fanning himself with a magazine, watching the same reports repeat on CNN and then running through the cable channels—Belgian, Dutch, German, French, finding nothing that held his interest, not the dubbed sitcoms or the subtitled American movies, the French discussions, or the bicycle race. He snapped the screen blank and waited in darkness until it was time to go to bed.

This night he did not expect to sleep, propped up with a pillow against the wall, tabulating the night sounds that entered through the open window—three rattling trucks, five scooters, a siren in the distance, a group of chattering people (perhaps the group from the restaurant), children calling to one another in a high-pitched French (What were they doing out so late? Were their silent parents with them?), a steady rumble of traffic, cars badly in need of tune-ups.

Lewis felt himself drifting, his breathing soft and slow, a pleasant sensation of sinking, his eyes closing, sliding down on the mattress.

Then a strange, screeching noise made him jump up with his feet on the floor, so abrupt he felt dizzy, not sure how much time had passed—seconds or hours. The noise was shrill and metallic. It could have come from a machine, or it could have been a human screech.

When he lunged to the window and pulled back the curtain, he saw nothing, just the empty street. He had expected blazing lights in all the houses, everyone stunned from their sleep. But only a very few apartments were lit, widely scattered, dim glows behind thick curtains. Perhaps he had dreamed it.

Lewis waited, held his breath, but he did not hear the sound again. Moments later a man whistled through his teeth, crying out what sounded like "Bent," as if calling for a person, the voice harsh, urgent, the intonations strange, certainly not French. Then again, furious, a garble of sounds, "Bent" the only word Lewis could make out.

Outside in the morning, Lewis saw a group of people milling on the sidewalk ahead—housewives, school children, men in business suits. The blue dome light atop a police car circled rapidly. An ambulance idled at the curb with rear doors open wide, inside stainless steel glittering in the sunlight.

He joined the crowd milling around the remnants of the bed frame and asked a woman what had happened. She was middle-aged, hair in curlers, wearing an apron over a navy blue bathrobe. "Le meurtre," the woman told him, grimacing, shaking her head. Murder.

"Who? When?"

110

She shrugged and turned away to stare at the door of the building where yesterday the old Arab woman had sat to play with the child.

Lewis waited with the others, shifting his briefcase from hand to hand, aware that he would be late for his first meeting. The police, he would explain. The police were blocking my street.

When two men in uniform carried the body out on a stretcher, the face covered with a white sheet, he saw from the black dress and the thick black shoes that it was the Arab woman. He wasn't surprised. Although he had no idea who else lived in that building, he had assumed it was her as soon as he saw the crowd, her withered face vivid in his mind, contorted with fear as she screamed in the night. Lewis wondered who was caring for the child, why the people inside the building weren't wailing their grief.

When the ambulance drove off, the others scattered, and Lewis walked toward his meeting, stopping to look back at the policemen standing by the door.

At the EU office the officials were gathered around a conference table, hands folded on the polished wood, clearly annoyed by the waiting. Lewis apologized and said no more, suddenly feeling foolish at the thought of wasting their time with a story of violence on a mundane street. These people devoted their days to scrutinizing printouts thick with figures, planning projects that would matter to half a continent. What would they care for an insignificant old woman from some downtrodden country?

But at the first break, while the others drank coffee from a China service, he ran down to the kiosk outside for the local papers, scanned them with his Berlitz French, looking several times before he found a small item on a back page. It told little more than he already knew, only the woman's name and age—Houda Zeiden, 78. A body was discovered. Knife wounds. No family was mentioned. Perhaps the child was not a granddaughter, no relation at all. Why had the woman been in Brussels, Lewis wondered, a stranger, displaced from her real home, with no meetings to fill her days?

Anton, one of the Dutch representatives, a tall tanned man with a red mustache, sat in the chair next to Lewis. "What could be so interesting in a local newspaper? Don't tell me you're already playing the market?"

Embarrassed, as if it had been some fault of his, Lewis told what had happened: the screech, the police on his street, the body.

Anton took the paper from the table. "It doesn't say anything about robbery."

"It says very little about anything."

"Possibly they know nothing more."

"That's sad." Lewis shook his head.

"Many things are sad." Anton folded the paper, pressed down the creases, as if sealing it shut.

On his way to the apartment Lewis stopped at the grocery, selecting three large peaches from a crate and a bottle of wine from a shelf inside. As the grocer counted out his change, he asked on an impulse, "Did you know the woman who was killed? Did she shop here?"

The man glared at him. "Many people shop here."

"Did she come in with a child?"

"I don't know anything. I don't want trouble." He pushed the coins across the counter and turned his back.

Lewis saw that a policeman still stood outside the door and hesitated before approaching him, fearing hours of interrogation as the price of his curiosity, meetings missed, a failure to accomplish what he had come for. "I live in that building." He pointed down the block. "I heard a noise last night, about 2 a.m. I think it was a scream."

The policeman nodded. "We've been told that." He was a plump man, red-faced, his uniform too tight, dark with circles of sweat.

Lewis waited, expecting questions, but the man just glowered, as if he hated this duty. Finally, Lewis said, "Do you want to ask me anything more?"

"That's the business of the detectives. My job is to stand guard."

"What happened to the child?"

The policeman shook his head, annoyed. "I've seen no child."

Lewis ate in, warming a canned stew, reluctant to heat the kitchen on such a night but unwilling to dine alone at a restaurant again. He had cooled the wine, sitting at the table with his fingers clenching a stemmed glass and staring at the grey blankness of the TV screen.

He thought of his son and daughter, years past two, on the verge of adolescence, with straight brown hair like his, very different from the dark curls of the little girl. But he remembered playing with his own children when they were babies, rolling a ball across the lawn, sitting like the old woman while they fumbled with pudgy fingers.

Later, in bed, he stared at the open window, wondering what would happen if someone climbed up the side of the building, a man with a knife who would hover over his sleeping form and then slash out. But why? He had nothing anyone would want, just a suitcase's worth of clothing and a briefcase of tedious documents. But what did the old woman have? All he had seen was a little girl and a brightly colored toy.

Back home his family, he knew, was safe, protected by a five-thousand-dollar security system with sensors at every door and windows, an alarm that would sound in the police station at the slightest disturbance.

This night felt even hotter than those before. He stripped the bed to the bottom sheet and sprawled naked in the darkness, alert to all the night sounds, expecting something terrible to happen again.

His memory of the screech was loudest of all, replaying again and again, more dreadful each time he heard it. Then the man's coarse "Bent," a sound pitiless in recollection. And he knew now that he had heard the voice of the murderer.

The next morning, very early for his meeting, Lewis sought out

Anton, took a chair in his tiny office and turned down the offer of coffee. Although Anton was a cordial man—all of the people here were cordial—he knew his company would be displeased to learn he had mentioned the crime again. But he found it necessary to talk.

Anton smiled, stirred sugar in his cup. "I thought America was the land of murders. Every time I'm there I see nothing else on the television."

Lewis shook his head. "Not where I live. All that's miles away from me."

"And so you had to come to Europe for violence on your street."

"He said, 'Bent.' The murderer did. Why would he say, 'Bent'?"

Anton folded his large hands on the desktop. "The woman, the victim, she was Arab?"

Lewis nodded, and Anton swung his chair to gaze out the window, thinking, flicking his tongue againt his teeth. "It wasn't bent," he finally said. "It was Arabic. *Bint.*" He repeated the word, enunciating carefully. "*Bint.*"

"And what does it mean?"

"Little girl. A child. Feminine."

Lewis winced, as if struck with a blow.

Lewis was gasping, sweat drenched; he had run all the way from the office. A sharp pain tore through his chest, his throat burned, a knee ached from his tripping on the gravel of Square Marguerite, tearing his trousers.

The same policeman as yesterday was guarding the building, slouching against a wall, not bothering to stifle a yawn. Although he did not greet Lewis, he gave him a look of recognition.

"I know," Lewis blurted, and paused to gulp air. "I know why she was killed." The policeman gave him a curious stare. "Someone, men, killed her for the child. They abducted the little girl. Bint."

"Yes. The detectives have that information."

"Then what are you doing about it?"

"The men and the child are probably far away by now. In

114

another country."

"Are you saying that nothing can be done?"

"People like that—they kill one another."

"But not here," Lewis insisted. "Not in Brussels."

The policeman shrugged. "It's not like that any more."

Lewis turned abruptly and walked back to his meeting. They must have started without him this time, irritated at his lack of concern, people of sincere good will, devoting their lives to a new Europe, an age of fruitful cooperation.

Someday their headquarters would be repaired, habitable, filled with the bustling of earnest officials. But all Lewis could hear as he stared at the empty building ahead of him was a screech and the echo of *"Bint, bint, bint."*

Saving Cimini

Cimini and Lukacs sat at a metal-topped table against the railing by the water's edge, Lukacs with his back to the lake, wrapping a napkin around his middle finger, scuffing his heel against the cobblestones. Cimini, unmoving, gazed out at the boats gliding across the glistening surface and beyond them at the lush Swiss hills on the far shore.

"Where, exactly, do you suppose the border is? A line on the water. Italy here. Switzerland there." Cimini pointed first to one spot on the water, then another.

Lukacs would not follow his eyes. "What's the difference?"

"It could be a matter of life or death." Cimini broke into a grin.

"I've known you for years, Cimini. You don't have to put on a performance for me."

"Perhaps I'm trying to disguise great fear." He threw his head back as if to laugh but made no sound.

Lukacs noticed the young woman at the next table stealing looks at Cimini despite the fat baby squealing on her lap and the small girl clinging to her knees. She was dark and broad-shouldered with thick lips slightly parted. Her legs were crossed, her short white shirt risen up on her thighs, a loose sandal flapping against the sole of her foot as she flexed her toes. The husband, very thin, his gaunt face overwhelmed by round spectacles, didn't seem to realize his wife was coveting another man. Or perhaps, Lukacs thought, he was just pretending.

Women were always staring at Cimini's face and he never noticed. The shape of his head seemed cast in bronze—broad tanned cheekbones and a hawkish nose, dark curled hair and a rich mustache, a strong jaw, a powerful torso.

He awaited the woman's reaction when Cimini stood up and she looked at the scrawny legs and flat buttocks. Cimini was shaped as if he had once suffered a severe wasting disease in the lower half of his body. Each time Lukacs saw the man again—emerging from a crowd, stepping out of shadows on a narrow street—his stomach wrenched at the sensation of something missing.

"I am grateful that you are willing to take me in your boat." Cimini's brown eyes overflowed sincerity. But Lukacs refused to meet them, to allow the man to drown him in mock gratitude.

"We have friends in common," he said.

Cimini pressed Lukacs's fist against the tabletop and spoke with an urgent hush. "Now, at this moment, I have no friend greater than you."

Lukacs yanked his hand free. The man's intensity infuriated him, as if they were merely playing a game with no consequences. For his own sake, Lukacs knew he could not make a move that was not anchored in urgency. In two hours it would be over, and once again for as long as his luck held he would have Cimini out of his life.

Lukacs looked up and caught the woman's eyes fixed on Cimini's profile. Startled by the contact, she quickly turned away to attend to her children. The girl was trying to climb on her lap with the baby. The woman spoke abruptly to her husband, and he stood to lift the girl into his arms. The child cried out and kicked her feet, almost knocking the tray of red wine bottles from the shoulder of the passing waitress. The waitress stumbled as she ducked away but regained her balance before the bottles fell. The father shook the child in rebuke and muttered apologies. The waitress frowned, a rough-faced woman with wiry yellow hair who stopped traffic with an outstretched arm each time she carried a tray across the town square from the restaurant's kitchen to the tables on the quay.

The three Frenchmen at a corner table above the lake nudged each other and smirked. The wine was for them, another serving.

"They're drunk," Lukacs said.

"Who?" Cimini turned his head and for the first time saw the family at the next table, the blushing mother, the scolding father, the sullen child struggling against his grasp. He gave a puzzled expression.

"Over there. The French." Lukacs gestured with his head. "Or they're very good actors."

The three, men in their thirties, bare-chested and newly sunburned under their sailing caps, tilted chairs back against the railing, their table top littered with plates and empty wine bottles. They had been eating and drinking when Cimini and Lukacs arrived, and now they were only drinking.

"I envy their pleasure," Cimini said.

"They're ridiculous."

"Aren't you ever tempted by frivolity?" Cimini asked.

One of the Frenchmen lifted an empty bottle out high over his head and splashed it into the lake. The others laughed aloud.

"That's not happiness," Lukacs said. "It's idiocy."

A second Frenchman threw two bottles at the water, simultaneously, one from each hand, and the third turned crimson, sliding down in his chair until his face pressed the cool metal of the table's surface. They were once muscular men whose bulk was turning to flab, sweaty pink flesh hanging over the waists of their shorts. The first, seeing that the waitress was across the square inside the restaurant, began tossing silverware into the water—a soup spoon, a fork, knives.

Two Italian policemen out on the pier noticed the Frenchmen. They stood together in discussion, gesturing their heads in the direction of the quay. Although they were only border guards, unarmed, stationed to check passports of people debarking the lake steamers, Lukacs spoke between his teeth. "Police. Face me. Show them the back of your head."

Cimini shrugged. "Save your worry for later."

The waitress stood above them, so suddenly that Lukacs nearly knocked over his cup. She ignored him and spoke to Cimini. "Dessert? A brandy?"

Cimini shrugged. "Why not a brandy?"

"We have a long drive ahead," Lukacs told her, shaking his head.

"A brandy never hurts," she said. Cimini winked at her, and she patted his shoulder as she moved toward the traffic.

"That wasn't smart," Lukacs said.

Cimini ignored him and gestured out toward the square. "The border is only a few hundred yards into those trees, and yet Italy is another world from Switzerland. See how fast they drive here, in the middle of the town. And the waitress walks right in front of them." He smiled again. "Maybe that's true heroism. A mystery to us both."

Lukacs would not respond. "And no sidewalks," Cimini continued. "The road comes up right against the buildings. They forgot to make room for people to walk, only for cars to drive. But in Switzerland everything makes sense. Everything is orderly."

"Is that why you want to go there?" Lukacs asked, even though he knew the real reason had nothing to do with order.

Cimini sat silently gazing out toward the villages on the Swiss shore, the stone church on a hilltop high above the stuccoed houses, the white yachts aligned at their moorings.

The baby began to cry and the mother cradled it in her arms. The Frenchmen were laughing again. Lukacs heard another loud splash and glanced over at the policemen. They were still watching, in close conversation, as if debating whether destruction of dinnerware was their responsibility.

One of the Frenchmen brought a bottle to his lips and toasted Cimini. When Cimini returned the salute, Lukacs kicked his leg under the table.

"Play the fool when you're alone," Lukacs told him. "When we're together I'm at risk too."

"Everyone is at risk." Cimini gestured out toward the tables and the lake and the green of Switzerland. "Do you think this is real life? The glowing sunlight, sails mirrored on a gentle lake, a family out for a Sunday excursion, young men having a drunken party? It's like a dream, a very pleasant dream."

"Are we more real?" Lukacs said. "Sitting here, waiting for darkness?"

"Have you ever lived in Germany?" he suddenly asked.

"Of course."

"That's right. I've forgotten that you've lived everywhere."

Lukacs couldn't judge his tone. It wasn't like Cimini to be sarcastic.

"During your time there, were you ever in a concentration camp?" he said.

"Of course not. That was decades ago." Lukacs had no idea what he was after.

"I tried to visit Dachau once."

"Yes?"

"I went on a Monday."

"So."

"They've turned the camp into a memorial. Like all the other public monuments, it's closed to visitors on Mondays." Cimini shook his head. "These days you can't get into Dachau on a Monday." He smiled broadly as if very amused.

"And?" Lukacs squeezed his fingers down on the edge of his chair, refusing to let the man see how furious he was.

"Some people want to pretend the whole world is Switzerland."

A Frenchman stood and lifted his chair, swinging it in a circle above his head. His friends thought he was hilarious; but he just dropped the chair back down under him and sat again, very pleased with his antics. Cimini was laughing too, the young woman smiling, though her husband pressed his mouth shut in a thin line.

A squat old man in baggy trousers staggered toward the Frenchmen, his face swollen with red veins. He braced his hands on their table and spoke a slurred Italian. The Frenchmen leaned forward and stroked their chins.

"He's telling them not to throw things in the lake," Cimini said.

"I know. I can hear."

When the old man turned and stumbled toward the waitress, one of the Frenchmen tossed a plate in the water, and the three put on innocent faces. The old man was trying to make the waitress understand what they were doing, pointing and waving his hands, clutching her arm and trying to pull her toward their table. She slapped him away and scolded. "Don't bother my customers. Get away from here, you old goat."

Cimini lifted his hand as if to call the waitress.

"Idiot!" Lukacs whispered to make him stop.

"I don't like them mocking him. They're drunk too."

"Just today. He's drunk all the time."

The young woman parted her blouse to nurse the baby, its head deep in the folds of the cloth, and now the husband was looking from Lukacs to Cimini, openly watching their table. Lukacs tried to see if he was somehow signaling the Frenchmen. Around Cimini anything could have meaning, even a child at its mother's breast.

Cimini leaned forward, inches from Lukacs. "You don't believe in what I do. Why are you helping me?"

"I have a boat," Lukacs said. "I cross the lake very often. No one suspects me."

"But everyone suspects me, and here you sit exposed in the open with a suspected man."

"I was asked."

"And do you do everything you're asked?"

"When certain people do the asking. Then I have no choice."

"They pay you very well for having no choice." Cimini displayed strong white teeth.

"Do you know how much I hate you?" Lukacs said.

Cimini nodded.

"I have no life. I spend my days expecting another message telling me to help you. The mail, the phone, a stranger on the street. Anything could be a signal about you."

"I don't think about you," Cimini said. "You are a man with a boat willing to take me to Switzerland. Nothing else is important—just moving me from this shore to that shore."

"My life matters!" Furious, Lukacs slapped the table, the metal ringing out over the lake, then with a sudden fear looked out at the others.

The Frenchmen were staring at Cimini, the three of them with hands gripped on the railing. They had stopped laughing. A chill pierced Lukacs. Perhaps they weren't drunk at all, the bottles and silverware merely props in an act. They had been sitting here before Cimini and Lukacs chose this cafe, so they couldn't have been following; but others like them might be stationed throughout the town, Cimini's face burned into their memories.

The Frenchmen slid back and stood to put on their shirts, pushing their arms through the sleeves. One of them seemed to nod at the father. Lukacs was sure of it. He swung his head around and saw the mother and children were gone, she halfway across the cobblestone square hurrying toward the restaurant, the baby tucked under one arm, the little girl clinging to her other hand.

When the father reached inside the plastic bag of baby supplies, Lukacs clutched his chair with both hands and tensed his knees. Now the Frenchmen were watching the father. Although the day remained brilliant, Lukacs felt his lungs burning, as if the oxygen had suddenly evaporated. He couldn't see the policemen; they were no longer on the pier. Cimini seemed calm, eyelids lowered, as if thinking of something far from these tables on the water. But his fingers were slowly creeping inside his jacket.

The Frenchmen moved forward in unison, then paused as if counting under their breaths. When the father began to withdraw his hand from the baby bag and they stepped toward Cimini, Lukacs kicked over his chair and bolted toward the square, colliding with the waitress, knocking her backwards against a car. The tray flew from her shoulder.

The detonations may have been gunshots or bursting glass. All sounds were jumbled in the din of crashing bottles and horn blasts and human shouts that jarred Lukacs's brain. He didn't look back, afraid that he would see Cimini standing on the quay, mocking him, his face alive with laughter.

Little Life

Morning dew seeped through the knees of Sylvia's slacks as she crept under a rhododendron looking for Stephanie. She hadn't been up this early in years, awake most of the night for fear she'd miss the alarm. Maybe it was too early. Most mornings when she went down to turn on the coffeemaker, Stephanie was meowing at the sun porch door, rubbing the frame when Sylvia opened it, yawning with hunger. But that was at seven. Now it was just six, the sun barely rising. But Sylvia had been nervous about not finding the cat on this day ever since the shelter finally called with news of an opening.

Alan knew she would have loved to keep the cat, make a pet of it. But his allergy was terrible. The one time she forgot and touched him after stroking Stephanie, his face swelled and his eyes reddened with a sneezing fit. No way could they have a cat, and Sylvia decided it wasn't right to make the poor creature live outside even though she fed her twice a day. For the first month after the cat appeared in their yard, it fled every time Sylvia stepped outside and called, "Here kitty, kitty." Eventually, the food did it, the certainty of regular meals. Sylvia even reached a point where she could pick it up, the cat almost weightless, purring loudly, desperate for affection. It deserved an indoor home with a family, pampered by children. But first she had to catch it and get it to the no-kill shelter.

If he had been here, not in Denver on a business trip, Alan would have helped her, wearing gloves, taking an antihistamine. But he couldn't pick the timing of his assigments.

"Stephanie," Sylvia whispered, made kissing sounds. "Please, Stephanie."

A noise made her look up, the slamming of a car door. Sylvia stared into the sunrise and saw a shape in the golden glow, large and square in the driveway. She scooted back around the bush to change her angle, touched her hand to her forehead to shade her eyes. It was Benny's van, a rusting gash the length of the passenger's side, a plastic sheet still taped up where the missing back window should be. But Benny was supposed to be seven hundred miles away, working. Why hadn't he called? Why was he there? On this day when she had to catch a cat.

Instead of Benny, standing in the driveway was a tiny thing that looked like a child. The sun dazzling her, making her dizzy, Sylvia stood up and stepped closer. It wasn't a child but a very small woman in shorts and a tanktop, her legs stocky, her pale face like a flexed muscle, cheeks bloated, two small eyes peering out directly at Sylvia.

Before Sylvia could ask her who she was, Benny came running around the front of the van and swooped Sylvia off her feet, spinning her and planting wet kisses on her cheek. "Mom! Mom!"

He was on a high. She knew it immediately. When he got manic like this, he sputtered meaningless sounds of excitement. What had happened to his therapy, the doses of Paxil and Wellbutrin? He'd been doing so well, promoted at work, engaged to Vicki. Benny was laughing as he clutched her, Sylvia moaning despair.

"Mom! Guess what!" Benny stepped back and seized her hands in his, turning a circle as he danced around her. "Guess what!" The way one shirttail hung at his side, the way his stomach hung over his belt, she could tell he was getting fat again.

"I can't guess," she told him, her voice flat with an old weariness.

"I'm fucking married!"

"Married? Where's Vicki?"

"Not Vicki. Daphne." He repeated it more loudly, with a sudden anger that she did not understand.

Benny rushed back to the girl in the driveway and dragged her toward Sylvia, pushed her against his mother. The girl just came up to Sylvia's chest, hands at her side, looking up with unblinking eyes.

Although Benny had forced them tight against each other, they were not really touching.

Sylvia looked down on Daphne's head, the purple streak in the cropped brown hair. "Are you really married to my son?"

"Benny woke up the justice of the peace. Banged on the door. The man wasn't happy, but he did it." The girl spoke in a monotone, barely audible.

Sylvia pushed her away and clamped Benny's face in her hands. "What's going on here? What about Vicki? We've been planning a wedding. Her mother and I talk all the time."

"The fucker's cancelled."

She wanted to hit him but held herself still. "Benny, when did you stop taking your pills?" It had to have been abrupt. People couldn't just stop. They had to taper off. Stopping would make them crazy. Benny was crazy. Her first thought was to call Alan, then decided it wasn't fair. He had his meetings. What could he do so far away? He wasn't Benny's father, and he had done more than enough to help her through her son's episodes for the fifteen years of their marriage. Alan had been so happy about Vicki. He would be crying right now if he knew.

"We both stopped." He wrapped an arm around Daphne. "That shit's no good for you. Daphne read about it. We walked out of group therapy one night and threw those fucking pills into the sewer. And we haven't been apart ever since. I said, 'Let's get married,' and we fucking did."

Benny threw his head back in laughter, rubbing wide circles on Daphne's back. The girl barely moved, almost comatose, Sylvia thought. But she was the one who raised her arm and pointed toward the shrubs—"What's that?" —startled as if she had never seen a cat before.

It was Stephanie, black and white against the green bushes, meowing, looking at Sylvia with what Sylvia knew was longing. She wanted to be picked up and cradled. Sylvia reached down and spread her hands under the cat's soft middle, lifting it to her chest, bringing her chin down to the fur of its back, swaying back and forth. The cat purred and Sylvia's tears beaded on the top of its head.

"What the fuck is that?" Benny was laughing, shaking his arm as he pointed.

Sylvia saw a thick ring on his fourth finger, but it wasn't a wedding band. "This is Stephanie." She hugged the cat tighter as if her son was about to rip it away.

"So you're trying to kill Alan. Have him choke on an allergy attack." Benny forced gagging sounds, staggered in a swoon.

"I wish I could keep her." Sylvia's voice trembled with sorrow. But if she didn't deliver the cat to the shelter this morning, she would lose her place on the waiting list. She broke into sobs.

"Mom. It's just a cat."

Tear-blinded, Sylvia realized Daphne was staring at her. She expected the girl to say something too, words that would echo her son's. But all she did was stare.

When Sylvia stopped crying, she carried the cat to the shelter's cardboard carrier by the sun porch, knowing how much she would miss the little face waiting outside the glass door every morning, head cocked, tail straight up. She brushed her lips to the small head and felt a sinking within.

The allergies weren't Alan's fault, and he had cared for her enough to marry a woman with a troubled teenager, shared in the counseling sessions and the boy's rages. Finally, they both believed they had succeeded, Benny clean, doing well in a good job, engaged to Vicki. But now! Sylvia wished there were a shelter that would take her.

With the cat in her arms, she couldn't unhook the tabs to open the box. "Help me," she called to Benny. He shook his head, still laughing. Daphne was the one, approaching slowly as if sleepwalking, saying something to Benny when she passed. Next to Sylvia, she dropped to her knees and spread the box top. Sylvia hesitated, not wanting to let go, but knelt to set Stephanie inside, surprised how docile the cat was, how it immediately curled and closed its eyes.

"Is it sick?" Daphne asked.

"Of course not. She's fine. She trusts me. Knows that I won't let anything happen to her."

"That's nice." The girl rose and drifted back into the yard near Benny. He wrapped his arms around her and lifted her off the grass, planting kisses on the top of her head.

Who was this girl? What was she doing here? Sylvia wanted her to vanish. Benny too. Both of them go back where they came from and let her think about the cat.

Without her realizing it, the day had become bright with morning light, lovely weather, a soft breeze, the scent of lilacs from the bush in the yard. When she looked toward the garage, she saw that Benny's van was blocking her in. She called to him and asked that he please move it.

"I'll drive you," he told her. "You're too upset. In no shape." That seemed to please him.

"And what kind of shape are you in?"

His face darkened. "I can fucking drive."

He put his hand against her back and guided her toward the van and slid open the gashed side door with a metallic creak. "Get inside." It was an order. He gave an abrupt wave to Daphne. "You too."

The girl opened the front passenger door and strained to reach the frame and pull herself up. She was that short. Benny took the carrier from Sylvia and placed it on the back seat. "Do you want a boost?" Sylvia shook her head and climbed inside. He slammed the door shut.

He started the van with a roar, tromping on the gas pedal. Dark exhaust clouded the rear window, crackling though a hole in the muffler. He burned rubber backing out the drive, but Sylvia wouldn't tell him to slow down. That would make it even worse. She knew Benny. Oh God, did she know Benny.

"So where's this crap shelter?"

She gave him directions, and in seconds he was speeding, swerving around corners, sending Sylvia and the carrier sliding across the seat. Her belt clamp was broken. She held the carrier, but the cat didn't make a sound. Sylvia tried to peek through one of the air holes but saw only a swatch of dark fur.

Her heart was pounding by the time they reached the shelter. Benny slammed the brakes in the parking area, cinders beating against the bottom of the van. She took deep breaths before speaking.

"You two can wait here. I want to do this myself."

"No fucking way. I want to see what this place is all about. Come on, Daph."

Would they turn her away after one look at her son and this dwarfish girl? She'd beg. Please find a family for this cat.

The young woman at the reception desk had a pretty face but several layers of chin fat and loose flesh swaying on her arms. She checked a computer screen and smiled at Sylvia. "There you are. On our schedule for today." She pointed to the carrier in Sylvia's hand. "And I'll bet that's Stephanie. Can't wait to meet her."

Sylvia sighed. Everything was going to be all right.

"Did someone explain the procedure?" the young woman asked, and went on even though Sylvia nodded. "One of our vets will examine Stephanie's vitals, give her rabies and distemper shots, and that'll be it. We'll check her in. Home sweet home."

They had to wait for the vet. Sylvia and Daphne took seats in plastic chairs, but Benny leaned over the counter watching the young woman's fingers on the keyboard with a wide grin. "You're sure some typist."

She didn't smile back. "That's why they hired me."

"Benny, sit down," Sylvia told him, and to her surprise he did, flipping though pet magazines, waving covers in front of Daphne's face. "Here's one called Cat Fancier. Can you believe this shit?"

Sylvia felt an urge to slap him, something she hadn't done since he was a toddler though she had wanted to hundreds of times. One more word out of him, and today she might actually do it. She opened the carrier to look down at Stephanie. The cat lay in the same curled position, the eyes closed. She had expected agitation at being taken to a new and strange place.

When the vet, a stooped man with thinning hair and a gray goatee, came down a hallway to call for her, Sylvia hoped Benny and Daphne would stay seated. But they followed at her heels, Benny pointing at the drawings of dogs and cats and rabbits that lined the walls as if he were seeing something very strange.

All of them crowded into the small treatment room, the vet spoke only to Sylvia, his tone businesslike. "Please put Stephanie on the table." She lifted the cat from the carrier. It lay limp in her arms, barely moved when she set it down on the stainless steel.

"You can see she's very docile. She'll be a wonderful pet."

The vet just pressed his lips tight and touched his gloved fingers into the cat's abdomen, brought his stethoscope down to the rib cage, then examined each of the four limbs. The cat lifted its head and gave a soft meow. The vet touched his goatee with the back of his wrist and wouldn't look at Sylvia.

"I'm afraid you have a very sick animal here."

"Sick? I've been feeding her for weeks. She had a great appetite."

"Look here." He spread the fur on the right hind hip to expose two small red scabs. "Those are bite marks. She must have gotten into a fight."

"With another cat?"

"With some wild animal. A cat. A raccoon. A woodchuck. Hard to tell."

"But you can give her a shot. Antibiotics."

The vet shook his head. "Whatever bit her could be rabid."

"Then give her a test."

"It doesn't work that way. State law says the cat has to be quarantined for six months."

"Six fucking months!" Benny blurted what Sylvia was thinking.

"I'm afraid that's the law."

"Can she stay here?" Sylvia asked.

"Afraid not. We don't have the facility. And we can't risk exposing the other animals."

"Then where?"

"You could board the animal at a special place. But that would get very expensive. Or you could keep her at your home."

"In that box!" Benny threw up his hands, shouting. Sylvia saw how agitated he was, on the verge of a real outburst. She held his arm, afraid he would throw her off. But he didn't. She knew it wasn't the cat that bothered him. It was rules, the threat of confinement. She looked back at Daphne with a pleading in her eyes. The girl stepped forward and stroked Benny's other arm.

"That's impossible," Sylvia said. "It would be so cruel."

The vet nodded. "I agree."

"Then what?"

"Euthanasia."

"Oh, my God." Her knees gave way, but Daphne held her up, surprisingly strong for someone so small.

"Can you do it?" the girl asked the vet, the first time she had spoken in that room, her voice soft and quiet.

"Yes. That's something we do."

"It's not right. It's not fair." Benny slapped the steel top of the treatment table, the sound ringing, but the vet ignored him and spoke to Sylvia.

"Some people like to be in the room. You have that choice."

Sylvia stood helpless. The day wasn't supposed to be this way. In bed, alone, too anxious to sleep, she had imagined Stephanie surrounded by children, stroked and purring, amid a family that truly cared.

It was Daphne who spoke again. "I don't think that's such a good idea."

The cat lay limp in the vet's arms as the man carried it out of the treatment room. When he was gone, Benny slammed the door.

Sylvia fell back against a wall, face quivering. "I loved that cat. I've never loved anything so much."

Daphne wrapped her arms around Syvia's waist and pressed her head against Sylvia's chest. "Her poor little life," she sighed. Sylvia clutched the girl and wept.

Awaiting the Night

Curtis took Eileen to Tuscany three months after her accident. No one had been hurt seriously, not Eileen or the family in the other car, though at times she complained of a fierce back pain that no doctor could diagnose. Eileen did not lose her license because the judge was a friend of their attorney, but she refused to drive, and her car sat in the garage after the body shop had smoothed the jagged edges of broken metal. She would wake up in the middle of the night, sobbing: "I could have killed them—the children." "No, you couldn't. You weren't driving fast enough," Curtis would argue, first sympathetic, then annoyed because she would not let it go. He knew, but did not tell her, that only luck had kept her from killing them all.

Through an agent, Curtis rented an apartment on a farm just minutes from a town called Buonconvento, living in what for centuries had been a granary, now renovated for *agriturismo* by the architect whose parents owned the land. From outside, the stone structure seemed no different from all the square barns spread across the landscape. But inside they had pure white walls under dark beamed ceilings, floors of cool Italian tile, sleek appliances in the kitchen, a TV and upright piano in the living room, a canopy bed draped with a sheer netting that shimmered in the breeze. When the architect threw open the door, Eileen had gasped and Curtis had cried out. "Fabulous!"

For the first days of their holiday, Eileen didn't want to leave the farm, nervous to ride in the tiny Fiat, her face so close to the windshield. Curtis made quick trips into the town for groceries at the Coop, produce at the Tutta Frutta, the unsalted local bread at the bakery. Though he was eager to explore the countryside, they spent hours sitting at the stone table on their patio looking out over the landscape. Each morning they would bring the carafe of thick bitter coffee outside and sip from espresso cups as the haze lifted from the fields. Behind them in the vineyards, a tractor moved slowly up and down the rows of grapes, the engine drone soothing in its constancy. In front of them, the wheat fields turned more golden with each sunrise, the red poppies brilliant in contrast. Birds sang in the shrubs; day and night the air was filled with song. Across a glen on the hillside of a neighboring farm, sheep bells echoed as the flock drifted from one pasture to another. Wherever they looked, out beyond the farm, they saw the Tuscan hills, undulations of brown and green, distant towns rising like monuments against the horizon. Everywhere a stillness and a world that glowed.

"This is perfect," Curtis would say a dozen times a day, aware how often he was repeating himself, but too struck by the wonder of it to care.

Each time Eileen would shake her head. "This isn't real."

It was Gerald, the man staying alone in the old tobacco barn at the edge of the wheat fields, who approached them at the end of the week to warn about the gypsies. He told them what to do if accosted. "Just hit out. Hit them even if they're children."

Eileen shuddered. "How could anyone do that?"

"You have to," Gerald insisted. "You can't think of them as kids. They're hopeless cases at six. Beyond rehabilitation. Who'd help them anyway? The parents train them to steal."

"Can't we just walk away?" Curtis asked, angry at the man for agitating his wife, angry at the gypsies for their existence in this world.

"They surround you. Gangs of them swarm all over you, grab at your clothes, pull at your bags, shove their hands in your pockets. You have to kick. Stomp. Elbow. Shout. Think of it as defending civilization."

From the look of him, Gerald hardly seemed a person to urge violence, frail and hunched, rimless glasses on a narrow, drawn face; a retired schoolteacher who wore long-sleeved dress shirts even in the midday heat. Curtis would have guessed him to be the perfect victim, not someone whose voice quivered on the edge of rage when he spoke of the gypsies, veins knotted across his forehead.

It had been the assault on a bus in Rome that changed him, the vehicle so packed he couldn't even bring his arms down to his sides. The two gypsy boys snaked toward him through the crowd, advancing from different directions, both small and dark, in sleeveless undershirts, stinking of sweat. Even though Gerald saw them coming, he had nowhere to move. The boys pressed against him, one at the front and one at the back. When he felt a hand on his wallet, he elbowed one boy in the stomach, brought down his shoe, hard, on the other's bare instep, "Scusi," he muttered when the second boy cried out. "Scusi!" Then he stomped with the other shoe.

"You can't imagine how good it felt," Gerald told them. "I've never hit anyone in my life before. But this was so satisfying."

After that Eileen didn't want to go to Florence, just stay on the farm or, finally, drive to the nearby hill towns, where the only people they met would be native Tuscans and blonde Germans loading wine into their Audis.

"It's nice here," she had said. "So beautiful and peaceful. We don't need cities."

But Curtis had insisted, sure people would think him a fool to miss one of the world's great cities only an hour away. "How can we be in Tuscany and not see Florence? We can't let stories about gypsies frighten us off."

"I don't want to hit children." She had stood by the car door, kicking at the stones of the driveway, tears streaming down her face.

"I won't let that happen," Curtis had promised.

In Florence, Eileen's fear palpitated as she pressed her purse against her middle with both hands, the strain knotting her face. The look of her made him nervous to pause before the gold shops on the Ponte Vecchio or the store windows on via de Zanetti, to stop to gaze at the Campanile or cross over to study the Ghiberti doors of the Baptistry. He let the crowds sweep them up, people speaking a dozen languages, urgently rushing from one site to another. Every place they walked, he watched for gypsies, sinister men, thieving women, swarms of corrupted children. He coiled the strap of his rucksack tight in his fist, alert for an attack from one of the narrow alleyways.

At the back of the Duomo, Curtis saw the gypsies, three women sitting on a low wall, barefoot, the hems of their dresses tattered, a pair that looked like sisters, bone thin, black hair matted, faces creased, red sores on their arms and legs. The fat woman between them must have been their mother. Surrounded by stuffed shopping bags, she wore a scarf knotted around her head and, despite the heat of the day, an unraveling grey sweater. A dark mole spread on her cheek.

Then the two boys raced past and tripped Curtis against the wall of the cathedral. "Hey! Goddamn it!" He clutched Eileen's arm to regain balance, then felt for his rucksack, anchored it to his side with an elbow.

The boys' bare feet slapped the stone pavement, their short pants torn, their skinny dark legs smeared with dirt. They stopped abruptly on the sidewalk to block a group of elderly women in floral skirts and white sneakers, pleading openhanded in nasal intonations. The women, tourists, looked at each other and reached into their purses for coins. The boys snatched them up and darted away without a gesture of thanks. They swerved toward two local Italians in flapping double-breasted jackets, who quickly chased them with backhanded swings, the flick of a cigarette end. The boys paused to jerk their arms in an obscene gesture, then disappeared around the apses.

"Somebody should do something." Eileen dug her nails into his wrist.

"Remember what Gerald told us," Curtis said. "They get beaten if they don't bring in a certain quota each day."

She made a face. "Who beats them?"

"The men."

But Curtis saw no gypsy men in sight, just the three women, surely the mothers and grandmother of the boys. Why here? Curtis wondered. Great crowds were milling in front of the Duomo, hundreds of people to beg from, pockets to pick. Then he remembered all the policemen there, clubs swinging from their thick leather belts, and understood why the gypsies had chosen this spot.

When the boys reappeared, rushing in his direction, Curtis stiffened and clenched his fists, about to swing out with both arms. But the boys veered toward an old man. When Curtis looked at Eileen, she shook her head, and he was ashamed of his urge.

"Let's go home," she said, and Curtis sighed with relief.

At the edge of the farm stood a large brown building, an odd structure with a square bell tower, a wide blank facade, and at the top a row of tiny windows. When Curtis inquired, Gerald explained it was a deconsecrated church, surprised that they hadn't known. Curtis asked what that meant, and Gerald said, "For years it used to be holy. Then someone performed a ceremony and now it's unholy." He repeated the word—*unholy*—and laughed out loud.

Gerald was leaving. They came out one morning and found him carrying suitcases down the steps of the converted tobacco shed that housed his apartment. He hadn't said anything about going when they had stopped to talk the day before.

Curtis and Eileen walked across the yard to the open trunk of his blue Renault, watched him maneuver a suitcase over bumper, then drag it out with a curse to rearrange its angle. Curtis offered to help, but Gerald shook his head.

Two cats approached in the grass, curious, expecting affection and food, a cream and white, pregnant female, the male with brown spots, perhaps a sibling. Gerald had fussed for hours over them, putting out bowls of milk, pulling string through the grass while they pounced, rocking them in his arms. But this day he ignored them, not reacting even when they rubbed against him.

"You didn't tell us." Eileen made sounds of disappointment.

"Oh? I thought I had."

"Are you leaving for good?" Curtis asked.

"Forever and a day."

Curtis expected Gerald to smile, but he reached for the other suitcase and lifted it with a grunt. "Where are you going now?"

"Venice," Gerald said. "It's someplace different."

Eileen hesitated. "Are there gypsies in Venice?"

"I have no idea. There very well may be."

"What will you do if there are?"

"The same thing I did in Rome—give them pain."

He slammed the trunk shut, started the engine, and drove out the dry dirt roads of the farm toward the town, his tires churning up a thick wake of dust. Curtis and Eileen stood watching until he disappeared. Curtis realized how much he disliked the man, disturbed by the fix of his eyes when he spoke of violence.

Eileen took to feeding the cats now that Gerald was gone. Each morning the animals were outside the door coiling in tight circles when she pulled back the bolt and opened to the new day. She set aside two cereal bowls for milk, invited the cats in, smiled at their meows as she lifted each one from the tiles and felt it purr in her arms.

Cloudbursts began to interrupt each afternoon—the bright sky suddenly vanished behind a grey mass, a brief hard shower, then the reappearance of the sun. The grass and vines would sparkle with raindrops and small puddles formed in the dirt. An hour later, the dusty heat of summer would return.

Curtis and Eileen took to staying indoors at the height of day when the rain fell. He remarked that they were becoming like the natives who shuttered their shops and their windows from noon till four. They found themselves napping, sprawled on the bed under the netting, the brightness shuttered out.

Lying side by side, both of them staring up at the slow turns of the ceiling fan, Eileen wondered about gypsies. "Why should people want to live that way? Nothing but parasites. For generations. For centuries."

"Once," he said, "people used to romanticize them."

"For God's sake, why?"

"Freedom. Nobody owned them. Nothing tied them down. They could pick up and move their camps on a whim."

"All they do is rob and steal. They don't earn anything. They ruin their children. They take beautiful cities and make them ugly."

"But they don't bother us here."

"I couldn't think of anything more awful." Eileen cringed.

In the long summer twilight, they walked about the quiet acres of the farm, following footpaths and tractor routes through the fields, taking the dirt road that passed over a bridge across a stream, curved through a grove of trees. Though the road went on for miles, they always turned back at the rush of water. They rarely saw another person, sometimes one or two workers in the fields who mowed wheat with long sweeps of their scythes. They could hear small animals rush through the undergrowth, the constant chirp of crickets, birds in the leaves.

More and more the old church out at the edge of the farm fascinated Curtis, the notion that such a thing as deconsecration was possible. How could a church stop being holy? He wondered if such a place could turn into its opposite. But he had no idea what that might be. Though Curtis was not a religious man, the possibility distressed him.

He found himself leading Eileen toward it during their evening walks when the sun began to set and the temperature dropped.

Two routes took them there, a narrow diagonal path across an open area of stiff grass and a diversion in the dirt road that cut through a field of dry corn stalks. A crumbling stone wall surrounded the building. Curtis never went beyond the gate. He would stare at the unkempt tangle of weeds in the courtyard and quickly turn back, relieved to get away. He wanted to say something to Eileen, but the strain on her face always made him stop. He couldn't bring himself to ask what troubled her.

He took to studying the building from his seat at the stone table during the day, moving to the window at night to see it outlined against the grey sky. He couldn't tell Eileen how much it disturbed him, like a shadow over the landscape. It's beautiful here, he kept telling her, upset at his inability to throw off his unease.

Though they rarely understood a word of Italian, Curtis and Eileen took to watching the television news. They had ignored the set the first week of their stay; but now he turned it on to fill the evening silence.

Something had happened in Brindisi—an explosion, photos of burning cars, the front of a building crumbled, naked rooms suspended from shattered beams, the urgent voices of the reporters, grave dark-suited politicians speaking into microphones. Curtis strained to make sense of the report. Was it an accident? Was it terror? He couldn't understand, and Eileen was no help, frustrating in her confusion. He snapped at her, then apologized immediately, unwilling to tell her that terrible things were happening and he had no idea what they were. Ambulances, sirens, terrified people with bloody faces. Eileen stood abruptly and turned off the set.

Curtis's sleep became troubled. He would awake in darkness, legs knotted in the sheets, then strain to read his watch, unable to tell the hour. He would lie listening to Eileen's openmouthed breathing, then await the other noises—a creak of the beams, something on the roof, footsteps. Night after night he was sure he heard footsteps, a pacing on the gravel, a hand tapping the wall.

Gypsies. It had to be gypsies. Prowling in the fields, stealing their way across the countryside. He imagined them living in the old church, dozens of them, the men who beat the children, hidden during the day, emerging at midnight to surround his apartment. If he got up and lifted the curtains, he would find sinister faces peering into the windows. But he couldn't make himself move.

In the mornings, the glow of daylight streaming into their rooms, the cats purring over their milk, these fears felt as vague as a distant dream. But Curtis knew they would return. He said nothing to Eileen and began to dread the dark.

At nightfall, a pink sky fading at the horizon behind the old church, Curtis stood out on the patio with an impulse to run out through the fields, down the road past the stream, not stopping until he discovered a different place. "Let's go into town," he told Eileen. "Let's get away from here for a while. Then maybe I'll be able to sleep."

They parked in a hedged field across the road from the town wall, directly opposite the gate of two huge wooden doors. When they passed through it onto the pedestrian stones of via Soccini, Curtis felt an emptiness, as if he had stepped into the vacuum of a suddenly deserted place. Faint lights glowed in the shop windows, and from up near a rooftop he could hear a distant music like sounds from a tiny radio.

"Where is everyone?" he said to Eileen, loud, just to hear his voice.

She shrugged, as if unwilling to answer.

"Isn't this strange?" he insisted, wanting her to speak.

"It's peaceful," she said. "Without people everything here is peaceful."

When they passed the window of the Ristorante Roma, Curtis paused to stare inside and saw only one couple at a table far in the rear, two waiters whispering at the door to the kitchen. He had hoped to find the usual people clustered at the two plastic tables outside the narrow bar across from the shoe store. But even they were empty on this night.

Eileen touched his arm and pointed up past the rooftops. "Look at the moon."

They stood in the center of the street gazing at the silver glow directly above them, wisps of cloud floating across its path. Then Curtis heard a metallic squeal and shouts, held his arms rigid and swiveled his head toward the source. A group of boys spilled from the alley between the tobacco shop and the butcher, two of them on bicycles, the others on foot running alongside. As they spread across the via Soccini moving toward Curtis and Eileen, they all yelled out in Italian, at the top of their voices, half song, half chant.

She ducked into a doorway, pulled at him to follow, but he stood his ground, slipped the rucksack off his shoulder. One of the boys on a bicycle glared at Curtis, rose from his seat and stomped hard on the pedals, heading directly for him. He knew the boy would swerve, that it was only bravado, but he swung anyway, gripping the strap of the rucksack and lashing out. It caught the boy on the shoulder, knocked him sideways. The bicycle skidded out from under him as he toppled back onto the cobblestones, his legs tangled in the frame, a shoe locked in broken spokes.

The boy's arm was scraped raw from the shoulder to the elbow, and his nose bled. The other boys clustered around him, helped him up, then surrounded Curtis screaming what he knew were Italian curses. He could feel his body shudder as he lifted the rucksack over his head and shouted. "Get away from me! Get away!"

The boys stepped back without another word and moved off down the street, helping their injured friend and pushing the two bicycles. The one the boy had been riding wobbled unsteadily. The others paused to look at Curtis and whispered to each other. Now bright lights blazed in the windows, faces peering from behind the glass.

In the car, Curtis sat with his hand on the ignition key, heart racing. He dropped his face to the steering wheel and took deep breaths, unable to make himself move. He could see Eileen's hands clenching and unclenching in her lap, faster and faster.

Then she was hitting him, her fists beating on his shoulders. "Let's get out of here! I have to get away from this place!"

"I didn't mean it," he said.

"They were only children! Children!"

It the middle of the night Curtis sat up in bed, cried out, and thrashed his arms, as if pushing some force away from him. Eileen turned on the lamp. "You've got to stop this," she said.

"Stop what?"

"This writhing and groaning night after night. I can't remember the last time I slept."

"I could have killed them all," he said.

For an instant, Curtis thought he saw hatred in her face, but Eileen propped herself up with a pillow, turned away, and opened a book. He squeezed his eyes shut and ached with fatigue.

Eileen wouldn't go outside. She accepted the coffee Curtis made and went back into the bedroom, caressing the cat on her lap and staring at the pure white wall. He tried to talk to her but got only curt one-syllable responses.

Curtis took his coffee out to the table despite the greyness of the day, the sky so thick he couldn't see past the edge of the farm, the old church barely visible in a dark fog. He sat imagining how he would travel into Florence to buy a new bicycle for the boy and deliver it back to the town. But he knew that was foolish. Who would he give it to? He hadn't really looked at any of their faces.

Curtis sat there into the afternoon, hungry but unable to make himself step into the kitchen. One of the cats, all brown but for a white throat, came out from a barn and walked up the path directly to him, sitting at his feet and meowing loudly. But when he reached to pick it up, it scooted back and lingered just beyond his reach.

The day turned black and a sudden wind swept across the patio, setting off a swirl of dust and leaves. He couldn't even see the next building now. Then there was a sound from above, a loud creak, as if the sky had split apart. Rain began to fall, hard and pelting, bouncing off the patio, churning the earth beyond the edge of the stones. The cat crept under the table. When Curtis bent down for it, it hissed and raked his arm.

Curtis held the arm out in the rain and watched the thin line of blood run down to his wrist, drip from his fingertips. The scratch began to sting; he felt it swelling. I should go inside, he told himself, put something on the wound. But after he stood, he couldn't make himself take the step.

The rain pounded against him, drenching his hair and his clothing, soaking his canvas shoes. Windblown, pounding, it stung his flesh. He turned his face up toward the sky and let it beat down on him, even when the hailstones started, large pellets that tore into the vegetation. The cat cowered, ears back, wet and trembling. Curtis felt an urge to cry out. Instead, he clenched his teeth and spread arms and legs, rooting himself into the stones.

Later, when it stopped, he wondered where Eileen had been through the storm, what she had heard, if she bothered to look out and see his battering. All around him shredded growth drooped against the soil. The air smelled of mud. Curtis felt the water running from his hair, under his shirt, like tears down his aching face.

In the evening, still hungry, Curtis asked Eileen if she wanted to walk, but she did not answer. Outside, the farm felt odd, as if it had endured an ordeal. Workers in the vineyard drove wooden stakes into the ground and tied up the sagging vines. The wheat sheaves looked trampled.

At the end of the path from his building to the dirt road, a square grey Fiat sat parked under a tree, all four doors, hood, and trunk lid wide open. Four young men, just teenagers, boys really, bent over peering into the engine. Curtis muttered a greeting when he passed, but they did not look up to acknowledge him.

The road was still hard even after the rain, but now and then he stepped into soft mud that clung to his shoes. When he brushed against bushes, the leaves left wet streaks on his shirt and trousers.

Curtis told himself he would walk past the stream and through the grove of trees, keep going until he saw what lay at the other end. Yet when he came to the path that led to the deconsecrated church, he could not make himself turn away. This night he would enter the courtyard, open the wide front door, and discover what lay inside. His pulse raced and a chill sweat spread over his flesh.

A horn sounded, a shrill bleating, once, twice, three times. The Fiat swerved onto the path behind him, moving much too fast, tearing out the undergrowth, a young boy leaning out of each window, banging the door metal with an open hand. They were shouting something, harsh words that didn't sound like Italian, making a raucous noise.

Curtis thought they must be drunk, and to let them pass he stepped into the cornfield, where the hail had shredded the stalks, tangled one atop the other. The car slowed to a creep when it came alongside him. One of the boys, his brown hair clipped close to his scalp, called out to Curtis.

When Curtis leaned forward to ask what he wanted, the young man sprayed his face with a thick foul liquid, then laughed, the four of them pointing and laughing. They tried to speed off, but a wheel spun in the mud.

Furious, blind anger pounding his skull, Curtis groped in the field for a large rock, lifted it with both hands and hurled it down into the windshield. A thousand cracks radiated from the impact like a live current. Then the car doors opened, and the boys jumped out, not large, but thickly muscled in their white tee shirts. They moved toward him, four abreast, walking slowly, saying nothing, fists cocked, mouths contorted. More rocks lay at Curtis's feet, but he did not reach for them. He stood with his arms at his sides, at last knowing what he had awaited in the night.

The Dream Vatican

It was Peggy's idea to tour the Vatican on their first morning in Rome. Edward found himself reluctant. He and Claire had flown four thousand miles to be with their daughter for the first time in a year, not to see the sights. Peggy was stationed in Turin as a strategic planner for her company's Italian subsidiary, and although her only visits since college had been occasional hectic weekends, Edward still missed telling himself she was accessible.

Through the overnight darkness of the flight, he recalled her eager girlhood confidences, her hands clutching his across a table, and imagined being able to make Peggy understand what was happening to his life. But from the moment they hugged at the airport, his daughter carried on a monologue of food, fashions, and office politics, pausing only to point out the buildings and monuments that whizzed past the taxi's windows; she announced an itinerary for the week ahead: art and antiquity, exclusive shops and fine restaurants. Edward sagged back in the seat, overwhelmed by her litany of names and places, finding few signs of his only child in this thirty-five-year-old woman who dressed in a European wardrobe and commanded porters in Berlitz Italian.

Now, a bright dawn glowing at the edges of their shutters, the Vatican scheduled right after breakfast, Claire suffered a migraine and lay in bed with a damp washcloth over her eyes and a prescription painkiller in reach on the night table. She wouldn't let Edward call Peggy to cancel, insisted that he not disappoint their daughter.

While he waited in the lobby, he realized that he didn't want to be alone with Peggy, that it had been folly to believe he'd be able to explain to her what he couldn't explain to himself. He would say, Whatever I do, it means nothing, and she would turn a bright light of scrutiny on his desolation, ask a dozen questions he couldn't bear to answer. Even though he knew he was being unfair, Edward resented Claire for abandoning him with their child.

When Peggy stepped off the elevator, she kissed his cheek and led him into the dining room.

"Where's mother?" she asked when they were seated.

"It's one of her headaches."

Peggy curled her lips. But Edward asked a question before she could speak. "Do you really like your work here?"

"Turin isn't Rome, and the office is so disorganized I want to scream. But I'm positioning myself. Doing my turn in the field. Then they'll owe me."

"What?"

"A career move."

"How much longer will it be?"

"A couple of years."

"That seems like a long time just to get a promotion. Aren't there other jobs in the company?"

She signaled the waiter for more coffee. "You and mother can't seem to understand—this isn't a punishment. They sent me here because I'm very good at what I do. You need international experience to advance, and I plan to be a vice president before I'm forty."

"Is that worth being away from home for so long?"

From the way she straightened in her chair Edward expected an annoyed response. But she only reached for a croissant and said, "I was in the States in April."

"But not home."

"Our meeting was in Kansas City. Morning till night. Then I had to rush back."

"When will you see Rachel?" The name sounded odd to Edward as he spoke it, here, in this hotel, as if it were as unfamiliar as one of Peggy's Giancarlos or Emilias. Yet when they were alone in their room Claire spoke of little else but their granddaughter, framed photos of the child turning her dressing table into a shrine. He said the name again. "Rachel misses you."

"Tell her Christmas."

"Don't you want to see her?"

"Of course I do." She twirled a spoon through her fingers. "But I'm the world's worst mother. I never know what to say to a three-year-old. She's much better off with Todd—and that girlfriend of his."

"Lisa."

Peggy gave a thin smile. "You know more than I do."

"Your mother worries about Rachel."

"She'll be fine. What Todd lacks as a husband he makes up for as a father." She drank the last of her coffee and looked down at her watch's black dial. "Time for the Vatican. We should finish before lunch. Maybe Mother's head will be settled by then."

Fifteen minutes later they stepped from a taxi at the edge of St. Peter's Square into a cluster of kiosks and pushcarts. Everywhere Edward looked he saw eager displays of holy artifacts: crucifixes, ceramic Madonnas, saints' medals, scarves bordered with the faces of martyrs. Vendors called in broken English, imploring them to buy as if their lives depended on it.

From the guidebook passages Peggy had read aloud during their ride, Edward expected the sweep of Bernini's colonnade to be breathtaking, but a tangle of tourists blocked the view, many on their knees focusing wide-angle lenses. A dismantled wooden platform lay to one side of the square like of pile of warehouse skids. People sprawled in a disorder of folding chairs; fatigued old women on the stone steps exposed layered undergarments and varicose veins.

"It's this way all over," Peggy said.

"How do you mean?"

"You hear about the wonders of the world your whole life, and every time you get to one, you find it's overrated."

"So why have we come?"

"After a year in Italy I figured I'd better see the sources of the postcards. All this" —she indicated the Vatican, and with a wave of her arm the sunlit city behind them—"is on its last legs. Pollution is eating the stone, traffic undermining the foundations."

"Then what?"

"Something different."

"But it's civilization," he said. "Our history."

"History is change. Layers of it are buried under our feet."

Before Edward could protest, Peggy took his arm and led him up the steps through huge bronze doors into St. Peter's, entering an immense space filled with statues and mosaics, tombs and altars, crowds of people, a clamor of echoes. Edward blinked the daylight from his eyes and strained to see.

Last night in a foreign hotel, jetlagged, the late dinner lying heavy on his stomach, a dream Vatican had emerged from the shadows of his mind: a maze of empty golden corridors, polished floors that rang with his steps. Alone, constantly meeting junctions, he had to choose from among several possible directions, always certain he was missing something of great value no matter which way he went. Tiny niches a hundred yards deep each radiated the brilliance of a single jeweled treasure. Huge rooms glowed with light and vibrated rich chords of sound. But, though no door or gate blocked his way, he could never enter. He could only stare at what he would never know and take more turns in the maze. At three a.m. he had awakened with a spasm in his middle, surprised because he had never once in his life thought about the Vatican before Peggy's schedule.

"Can't you sleep either?" Claire had startled him with her question, and Edward wanted to describe his dream as they lay in the darkness, wishing he could find words that would help him recapture the vividness. He reached out to touch her arm just as she slid up against the headboard and flicked on the nightlight.

"I can't face tomorrow," she had said.

"What? The Vatican?"

"Our daughter. She's so desperate."

"Peggy? All she thinks about is her career."

"Don't you understand how unhappy she is?"

What about me? Edward had wanted to cry. All of us? But he only closed his eyes and watched the unattainable beauty of his vision fade behind a shadow.

Peggy pulled him toward the Pietà, enclosed within a protective case ever since a madman had attacked it with a hammer. The plastic blurred the white sculpture as if it were under water. Tourists snapped pictures with glaring flashes.

She shook her head. "All they'll get are reflections in the plexiglass."

Guides led knots of people past them, pointing at the dome, at the mosaics, at the huge central altar with pillars hewed from cedars of Lebanon, chanting descriptions in a babel of Italian, French, German, English.

Two shriveled old women in black dresses, black shawls, black shoes dropped to their knees beside Edward and crossed themselves, tears streaming down the folds of their faces.

"This place is crazy," Peggy whispered, "everybody desperate for something to believe in."

One guide had tied a white handkerchief to an umbrella handle and waved it high over his head for his group to follow; stragglers half ran to keep up, pushing their way through packs of strangers.

So much was happening, Edward couldn't focus. It was nothing like the great glowing chambers of his imagination. A chaotic din rang through his brain.

He forced himself to concentrate on a large mosaic directly across from the spot where they stood, over the heads of all the people, Virgin and Bambino, the flesh of the baby alabaster white, halos of golden tiles surrounding mother and child.

Peggy saw him staring and frowned her annoyance. "Your dream of daughter Peggy and baby Rachel. The fullness of life."

"Actually I was thinking of your mother and you."

"The rules have changed, Dad. Todd and I analyzed our marriage to the point of tedium." She leaned back against a column. "What we did was for the best. He likes parenting. I like a career.

148

But you won't understand. One look at me and Mother takes to her bed."

"Jetlag," Edward said.

"It's some sort of lag." Peggy pulled him away, into the midst of a group crossing the marble floor, her eyes brimming tears. But Edward couldn't tell if they were from anger or sorrow. "Let's stop this," she said. "We're here to look at all the art."

Her gaze shifted from statues to paintings to frescoes, never lingering for more than a glance. He followed her, threading through the tangles of people, and stopped when she paused to peer down into a glass-topped casket. There lay the preserved body of a pope in holy robes, Leo XIII, 1810-1903. Edward turned away with a shake of his head.

She noticed his reaction. "Don't you think they're overdoing it?"

"I've never understood religion," he told her.

"It's clinging to what you thought you knew."

Edward clutched her hand and made himself speak: "I don't know which way to turn, what's coming next." But the glut of voices beneath the dome drowned his words. Peggy shook her head. "I didn't hear you."

When he tried to pull her close, the human crush forced them apart. She cupped her hand to her mouth. "There's no point in fighting the crowd. You find what interests you and I'll do the same. We'll meet out on the front steps in half an hour." She looked at her watch. "At 11:45." Then she was gone.

He stood bewildered for a moment, tried to study a painting but found his view blocked by two blue-haired American women in tweed skirts and foulard scarves. "A lady from Chicago was telling me," one said, "that the shops here sell statues and holy medals that are blessed by the Pope."

"How can he find the time?" her friend asked.

"At the end of each day they take all the things people buy to him. He blesses them all at once and your item is delivered to your hotel that evening."

Edward waited for some sign of an attitude. The woman had delivered the information so neutrally, as if it were just another oddity of a foreign land.

He found himself pushed to the edge of the others, standing in a dim corner by an obscure stairway to the crypt. He could see no other way out.

As he descended the stone steps, images from the dream filled his memory—rooms glowing with light, vibrating with magnificent chords. He trembled in anticipation, but the corridors ahead were only blank white marble, the narrow burial chambers illuminated with naked light, sterile. He paced along a route marked with arrows set into the floor and read the nameplates of the dead. Then he saw a weeping woman, elegant in silk, kneeling to place lilacs on a tomb. He studied the gesture, coveting her ability to name her grief. She glanced up and he moved away in embarrassment.

Back home whenever emptiness overtook him at his desk, he would drop his pen and turn to the framed photo of his family standing on a white beach against an absolute blue background, the three of them—father, mother, and a teenaged Peggy—arms linked and stepping toward the camera as if they were dancing in unison.

That morning as he was buttoning his shirt Claire had reached from the bed and seized his hand. "Talk to her," she had implored. "Tell her she has to believe in something outside herself."

"Were we ever really happy?" His question had been a plea, but Claire did not answer. He wondered if she had even heard.

Here, surrounded by the tombs of dead popes, a sense of his ignorance swept over him like a great dark bird. He imagined the white walls parting to reveal a distant glow in an endless passageway, the walls sealing behind him forever when he entered. He stopped with shivering legs and pressed his forehead to the cool stone.

A guard asked in fragmented English if something were wrong. "No, no," he said and moved on.

Another set of steps led up to the sunlight at a side entrance to the cathedral. The sudden brightness dazzled him, and it took him a few seconds to get his bearings. A small badly shaven man in a shapeless grey sweater was pulling at his sleeve. "You buy holy medal." He held out a velvet-lined tray. "Twenty Euro."

Edward crushed bills into the man's hand and reached into the tray, clutching the first medal he touched. "Is it blessed?" he asked. The man squinted incomprehension and moved away.

Peggy was standing on the top step by the great central doors in front of St. Peter's, glancing at her watch. Edward came up from behind so that she would have to turn to face him when he touched her shoulder.

"I have something for you," he said and pressed the medal into her palm.

"What's this?" She dangled the crudely stamped oval from its thin chain and gave him a bewildered look.

Edward knew she was awaiting his signal to laugh. But he would not offer it.

Power Failure

It was an odd sensation for Vincent, as if the world were split in two. Directly over the outdoor platform of the Montreux station where he waited for the 18:20 to Gstaad, the sun was bright, much too warm for his wool blazer; but the eastern sky was leaden with black clouds slowly thickening toward him. If the train did not arrive soon, he feared a huge drenching storm.

Vincent studied his watch as if he had set it wrong at the airport. Swiss trains weren't supposed to be late, and this one had been due twenty minutes ago. He worried that Marina, waiting at her hotel in Gstaad, would think he missed his train despite the precise timetable she had faxed him: the Geneva airport to Lausane at 16:58, from there to Montreux at 17:55, then Montreux to Gstaad at 18:20. Worse yet, she might think that he had changed his mind.

None of the others seemed concerned. A few people were peering down the line, probably strangers like himself. Most waited amidst their luggage and chatted. When children began to play on the track, the conductor made no move to chase them. Some people began to drift toward the cafe across the way. Vincent could see them gathering at tables. Every few minutes the loudspeaker broadcast an announcement and the people around him commented. But, ignorant of French, he did not understand a word they were saying.

There was obviously a problem, and Vincent, a man who was paid large amounts to devise solutions, began to pace in frustration. Overhearing an exchange in English, he edged toward a couple in matching shorts, cleared his throat, and asked, "Do you know what's happening?"

"Something along the line." The man shrugged as if it didn't matter to him. The wife nodded.

Vincent turned away, suddenly furious with them, as if it were their fault he didn't have control, that he could not just give the slightest nod to a secretary and have a limousine waiting in minutes. Here he couldn't even get a mobile phone signal.

The platform had gotten very crowded, more people still coming up the stairway, dragging suitcases and backpacks, even baby carriages and dogs, probably passengers who had planned to take the next train. Relieved that he had a first-class ticket, Vincent imagined them all jammed into coaches, babies screaming, animals howling, everyone gasping in the airless heat.

They all looked so slovenly. He had expected the Swiss to be neat, but he was surrounded by bare legs, old couples with thick tanned calves in hiking boots, parents and children in thin sandals, young people in tank tops, some of the males even bare-chested. Everyone looked unwashed. He was the only one in tie and jacket, his shirt newly laundered, clothing pressed for his weekend with Marina.

On the train from Geneva he hadn't noticed the others. Most of the first-class seats had been empty, spread wide apart, with high backs that gave privacy. Then he remembered there had been someone else dressed, an ancient man in a pale grey suit, but tieless, even though his stiff shirt collar was buttoned. Pink skin drawn taut over a hawk nose and a sunken chin, he had stared straight ahead and shuffled between a couple who looked like his daughter and son-in-law, two middle-aged people that Vincent recognized as contemporaries, the son-in-law tall and erect, with the bearing of a banker. Vincent scanned the crowd of waiting passengers for them and wondered why they had bothered to bring an old man like that out in public.

A train that had been standing beyond the station began to back up toward the platform, and Vincent joined the surge toward it. But it stopped with a metallic squeal and lurched forward to park on a different track.

He glanced at his watch again. By this time he should have

been halfway toward Marina. The plan had been for him to take a cab to her hotel, go directly to her door, and tap. He imagined her opening to him, richly scented, sheathed in a transparent gown that would part to his embrace. Once he closed the door, language wouldn't matter, nothing of the world outside that room.

His face was slick with sweat. Something was happening to the air pressure, the barometer plunging. He opened his mouth and tried to take a deep swallow, then felt prickles of perspiration under his shirt. The garment bag strap was beginning to cut into his shoulder.

When a sudden wind swept the newspaper from his hand, he moved back under cover and watched the open sheets scuttle along the tracks until a conductor wadded them into a trashcan.

Vincent found himself beside an elderly French-speaking couple, both grey-haired and richly tanned, the man in a sport shirt and the woman in a light print dress. The man was large and loose, with a broad nose and thick cheeks. They seemed to be arguing, speaking rapidly, the man's voice suddenly blurting phrases of disgust. But the wife just laughed and slapped at his hands. Each time he frowned and held out a paper sack so that she could take another plum.

Now it was dark as midnight, the clouds directly overhead. Far in the distance, streaks of lightning flashed over the mountains, but no thunder sounded. Vincent could smell rain, certain there would be a downpour soon, hoping for a soaking that would break the humidity. He decided to approach the conductor clustered on the track with two trainmen in orange coveralls.

"Will there be a train to Gstaad?" he interrupted, speaking with authority, as if the tone of his voice would force action.

One of the men glanced up. "Here." He pointed to the track. "If it comes."

When he passed the glass of a vending machine, he got a faint reflection of himself, face red and glistening, tie askew. He tightened the knot and patted his brow with a handkerchief.

He imagined Marina seated at a dressing table brushing her

hair, deciding which perfume to wear, the only light in the room a thin glow at the edges of the curtains.

They had met at a business meeting, her consulting firm, international in its reputation, hired to give his company a European image. He had opposed the idea, arguing that they shouldn't tamper with a century-old reputation; they weren't global anyway; they didn't need Europe to prosper. His assistant had warned him about the woman, her perfect French and Italian, the force of her grace. Then Marina entered the room, and he was stunned by her presence. She had sat next to him at the meeting and through the afternoon, while jotting quick notes with a thin silver pen, gave him private smiles, as if they shared a secret. After dinner, uncertain whether he had been offered an invitation or a challenge, he took her aside: "I'd like to see you again." She touched his face. "I'll be in Europe next week. Come to Gstaad."

The loudspeakers broadcast an announcement, this one longer than the others. The conductors were gesturing, and Vincent saw people hoisting luggage and descending the stairway from the platform. He joined the press of bodies flowing down into the passageway, assuming the train had been rerouted to a different track and that they would all turn toward another set of steps. But everyone moved out of the station into the street where a double-length bus sat parked against the curb.

Vincent stood bewildered watching the others board. A young woman, slight and dark, spoke to him in French and then in English. "The power is out. No trains. You should get on."

By the time he stepped inside, all the seats were taken. He stood in the aisle, shuffling backward as more people climbed through the doors. "Will this get me to Gstaad?" he asked a young man seated beside him. "Yes, yes, Gstaad." The young man, also dark, with thick black hair that spilled over his ears, was next to the young woman who had advised Vincent. She smiled up at him. "It's all right." Someone pushed against him and he found himself wedged behind their seats, his garment bag still over his shoulder. He let it slide off onto the floor behind him and put a foot through the strap.

155

Vincent realized that he was standing with one foot on a swivel pivot of the flexible vehicle between the two halves of the bus. There was no room to move, the space jammed with luggage, people sitting on suitcases, a girl in a sundress reading a thick book under the dim ceiling light. Across from him two women held a small boy across their laps, playing a game with Winnie the Pooh characters.

The others didn't seemed bothered by the stifling heat. But Vincent bent his head back in hope of a breeze from the open vent in the bus ceiling a few feet ahead of him. He tried to breathe deeply, draw clean air into his clogged lungs. Then the rain came, beating down with a sudden rush, and a man pushed forward to slam the vent shut. Vincent almost cried out for him to stop.

The bus began to move, slowly, thick in traffic on the glistening street. In seconds they had to stop at a red light. The side windows were already fogged, and he could see nothing but a blur of headlights. When they turned a corner, Vincent tripped backwards against the accordion side of the bus. He clutched at a seatback and pulled himself up.

The dark girl looked toward him, smiled, and held out her hand, as if to say what an odd predicament. She returned to her conversation with the young man, he doing most of the talking, serious, as if what he was saying was very important to them; she nodded and commented, clearly agreeing and making him more deeply expansive. Her face was thin, hollow-cheeked, eyes large and deep.

Vincent found himself drawn to her, as if they were friends after two brief exchanges. She couldn't have been past her early twenties, the man a few years older, probably her boyfriend, perhaps a fiancé. He liked the way they interacted, the frequent meeting of their eyes, not sensual, but familiar, sure of each other. Their words meant nothing to him, but it struck him that they were not speaking in French or Italian, certainly not German. It was a language he had never heard before.

The bus was out of the city now. There weren't as many

intersections, and the traffic moved more steadily. Vincent assumed they were on a highway. The rain had slowed but still drummed against the roof. The windshield wipers slapped back and forth, and a passenger was leaning over the driver, wiping the inside of the glass with a white cloth.

The little boy next to him kept crawling from lap to lap of the two women who played the Pooh game with him. The women looked like sisters, and it was impossible to tell which was mother and which was aunt. The boy burrowed against them and made them wrap him in a blanket while he thrashed and made odd chugging noises. It struck Vincent that the child was playing train in the tunnel. He kept twisting free and throwing off the blanket with a cry of triumph.

Vincent wished the women would tell him to stop. The high-pitched squeal was like a needle through his brain. Then several of the young people among the luggage began to sing, people around him clapping out rhythm. Vincent wanted to plead for silence. He leaned his head back against the accordion folds and felt a chill sweat under his clothing. When he closed his eyes, his head spun.

The dark girl was tugging at his hand. "Do you want to sit down? I don't mind standing for a bit."

"No. No. Thank you, no."

She gave him a glance of concern. When she took her hand from his, he almost clutched it back.

He wished he weren't alone, that he could turn to a companion and ask if he looked so sick, so frail that a young woman would feel compelled to give up her seat. He had a daughter her age, the child of his first marriage, now living across the country from him, reached only through holiday calls and a brief, awkward visit every year or two.

He was so hot, so starved for breath, he wanted to slide down the side of the bus and sit in a heap. But he wouldn't let himself. If he fought his weakness, he would be all right.

"Why don't you take off your jacket?" The girl had to repeat her suggestion before he understood that she was talking to him.

"It's very hot in here. Loosen your tie." She wore baggy shorts and a loose print blouse, her bare feet on the seat cushions, knees up by her shoulders. "It's best to relax on a night like this."

"Yes," he said. "Thank you." Vincent undid the tie knot, slid the silk from around his neck, and rolled it into a pocket; then he slipped out of his blazer, folded down the back seam, doubled it over, and placed it on his garment bag. "Yes, that's better."

He wiped the window behind him with his palm and tried to look out past the smear. But he could see nothing but a row of cars passing in the other direction. There were no lights on the landscape from what must have been farms and villages. Everyone had to live in darkness.

When the bus turned down a ramp, Vincent's knees gave way and he had to seize the seatback of the young couple. "Please," the girl said. "I really don't mind standing. It's not fair that you should be so uncomfortable."

"No, no. I'm fine."

He feared the young man would repeat the girl's offer, that he would not stop himself from accepting, sink down on the seat beside her and lay his head on her lap.

The bus pulled into a drive and stopped. The doors opened and, amid laughter and farewells, people gathered up their baggage to step off.

"Is this Gstaad?" Vincent said, suddenly afraid the bus would carry him beyond.

The young man grinned. "No. It's miles away with stops before. I'll tell you when."

Only a few people had left, their seats quickly taken. Vincent realized how many elderly people had been riding ahead of him all this time, the couple that had been arguing in French and sharing plums. Now he saw the ancient pink man in the pale grey suit, seated rigidly, gaze fixed out at something unseen past the windshield. The man was still impeccably neat, while his own jacket had become balled on the floor, his trousers wrinkled, his shirt half pulled from his belt. Vincent tucked it in tight, shook out his trouser legs, tried to pinch a crease back with thumb and forefinger.

His chest began to ache, a sharp pain under the left arm and down into his fingertips. A rancid taste filled his mouth. He knew it couldn't be a heart attack. Heart attack pains were different, he had once read. This was stress, indigestion, foul air. But the sensation was awful, as if he were dying. He imagined Marina at the side of the bus, blocked off from him by the others, yet witness to every move he made. I'm not that old, he wanted to tell someone.

Vincent let himself sink down to the floor, hoping the girl would peer back at him and show a face of concern. Come sit beside me, he wanted to say; come hold my hand. But no one noticed him.

The bus stopped a few more times. He heard people leave, the singing stop, but did not look up until the girl spoke. "There are many seats now. You don't have to be there."

"Oh, yes." Across from him, mother, aunt, and boy were gone. But when he tried to get up, his legs had no strength. The young man gripped him under the arms and lifted, half carried him over to the seat, then dropped his garment bag and jacket beside him. "You're not used to this," the young man said. "They must not have power failures in your country."

"No," Vincent said. "It's different there."

The bus was nearly empty now. They had been riding for several hours, the rain stopped but still no lights in the houses.

Vincent closed his eyes and imagined the girl on one side of him, the young man on the other. They would guide him home, to a place where he could sleep for days.

Then her voice was in his ear. "We get off soon. Gstaad is the next stop after ours. You're almost there. They have electricity. Power. It will be fine now."

"Thank you. Thank you for everything."

He watched them leave through the rear entrance, just one nylon bag between them. When the girl turned to wave, he pressed his face into his sleeve and wiped away tears.

Gstaad came only a few minutes later, a brightly lit town, dry, as if it had never rained there, the streets filled with people peering into glittering shop windows, stepping in and out of restaurants, greeting friends with cheerful embraces. Everyone seemed dressed in brilliant vacation outfits, moving with elegance and ease.

The bus stopped by the station, the doors slapping open with a hydraulic hiss, and Vincent was the last one out, one leg numb, stumbling when he stepped to the pavement. There under a streetlight Marina waited, absolutely lovely in pink, watching the bus with the edge of a smile, her hand in the air, ready to wave. She had left her hotel to meet him. But Vincent couldn't call out to her. He stood ashen, shirt saturated, blazer wadded under his arm, garment bag dragging on the ground. Marina gazed out intently, looked directly into his face, and did not see him.

Someone to Clean

When the hospice nurse came down into the living room to tell Mason that Virginia had died, his first thought was to call Lila and ask her to clean.   Even as he followed the nurse back up the steps to the guest room, he wondered why of all things that notion came into his mind when he had to inform his children and then the funeral home. He hardly knew Lila, rarely saw her during the ten years she had arrived once a week to scrub and polish for Virginia. She had been there the past Monday, sitting on the edge of Virginia's bed, speaking softly. From the hallway, Mason, working at home, had watched Virginia gaunt and ashen, barely nodding. Then the nurse came and Lila left without even dusting.

This nurse was a sturdy woman, hair cropped short, reading glasses dangling from a chain. At the doorway, she touched his arm, eyes soft with sympathy, but said nothing, just gestured toward the bed where she had pulled the covers up to Virginia's chin. His wife's mouth was open, jaw contorted as if she had made one last gasp for breath and froze in the midst of it. Had she wanted him to call Lila? Were those her last words, gasped to the nurse because he wasn't there to hear? He shook his head, aware that he was being foolish.

Mason phoned the children, miles away, forewarned and awaiting his message, two daughters and a son, the oldest first, the way he always did in an attempt not to pick favorites. They had visited separately a month ago, spending time alone with their mother, saying their goodbyes, and Mason gave them privacy. But despite the doctor's predictions Virginia had lingered, and Mason put off sharing his own farewell, wanting more time as he rehearsed the words in his head, not believing he would ever have to speak them.

This night the conversations with his children were brief, his gulp of hesitation and then, "She's gone." Soft sobs from both daughters despite the inevitable. He could feel them squeezing their phones, groping for words. He promised to give them details about the funeral tomorrow. "All right," they told him, both of them speaking in the same tone of voice. It struck him how alike they had always sounded. His son asked the exact time his mother had died, and that struck Mason as odd. He hadn't thought to look at his watch. The nurse would know. She was writing on forms in the next room, giving him privacy, but he could hear the tap of her pen.

While he waited for the undertakers, alone, the nurse gone to make another visit, he wondered if he really should call Lila, this stranger whose name had popped into his head. But she wasn't a stranger to Virginia, who spoke of her often, recounting their weekly conversations, shaking her head at the endless series of miseries in Lila's life. For all those years the day Lila was due to clean, his wife had left her work at the shop for an hour, a fifteen-minute drive to unlock the door, and then time to talk over coffee before she had to go back and Lila had to begin her chores.

"Do you consider her a friend?" he had asked Virginia once.

The question seemed to surprise her, "I never thought of it that way, but I suppose she is."

The word "suppose" echoed in Mason's memory as he opened a kitchen drawer and searched through Virginia's address book, realizing he didn't know Lila's last name. But there was her number, under L, as if Virginia had not known either.

The phone rang many times and he wondered if he should leave a message on an answering machine. How would he word it? Would it be better to wait until he could speak to her in person? But someone finally picked up the phone, slowly and clumsily. A voice said, "Huh," as if shaken from a deep sleep though it was still early evening.

"Is this Lila?" he asked.

The woman yawned before she answered. He imagined her mouth wide open, a pink palate. "Yeah. Sure. It's me." She had an accent he couldn't place, harsh, gravelly, something he had never noticed the few times he met her, unexpectedly home from the office.

"This is Mason," he said. "Virginia's husband."

"If she wants me to come tomorrow. I can be there."

"It's not that. There's something you should know. Virginia died today."

He expected murmurs of sympathy, a sad acknowledgment of the expected. Instead Lila wailed, a cry as if he had wounded her. She wouldn't stop wailing. He held the phone away from his ear and wanted her to stop. Then she intoned "Oh my God" again and again.

When she did stop, only a heavy gasping at her end, he had the sensation that he should be the one comforting her. "There was no hope. She was suffering so much."

Lila started again. "Oh my God, oh my God."

A tapping at the door relieved him. "It's the people from the funeral home. I have to go now." Ready to hang up, he said, "Can you come here tomorrow? I need your help." He pictured the mess in the guest room, plastic bags, bandage wrappings, wadded tissues, soiled sheets. He wasn't sure she heard him, was even listening.

But she said, "I'll be there," voice firm, definite, and she named a time as if she were the one with the right to decide.

The two men from the funeral home, probably a father and son, solemn, in dark suits, shook his hand and said words with practiced concern. He pointed up the stairway to the guest room. "It's on the left." And he realized he didn't want to go with them. He stayed rooted at the bottom of the steps and turned away when they came down with Virginia's body, the face covered with a sheet.

"I didn't want to see her like that," he said, as if he owed the undertakers an explanation. They nodded, and the older one left a business card on the coffee table.

Alone in the master bedroom, as he had been for months, Mason lay awake and wondered if asking Lila to clean had been a mistake. He might be very busy. The next day it turned out that he wasn't. His office didn't expect him. They knew about the situation. After speaking with his children about their travel plans and the funeral home about arrangements already made in advance, he had nothing to do. So he sat on the sofa alone in the silence, no sounds of dying from upstairs, no footsteps of the nurse. He looked at his watch and awaited Lila.

When Mason heard her shoes on the porch, he had a sudden fear that she would begin wailing again, a terrible noise he couldn't cope with. But she just stared at him when he opened the door, without a greeting or a word of sympathy. Her mouth was fixed, and she didn't move to step inside.

"Was this a mistake?" he asked her. "Too soon?"

The shake of her head was like a spasm. She pushed past him and went directly into the kitchen, rummaging under the sink for sponges and cleansers, her hands in yellow rubber gloves. He hadn't seen her put them on and wondered if she had arrived that way.

Watching her movements, Mason realized he didn't remember her clearly, really hadn't looked at her in Virginia's room just days ago. The Lila he expected was smaller and thinner. Here she dominated the kitchen with her bulk, not fat, just thick in the thighs and in the middle, her head large under a knot of dark hair, her tawny face attractive, or would have been on a different woman, someone who didn't set it in what seemed defiance.

Then he recalled all that Virginia had been telling him at dinner for years after Lila's weekly visits, her litany of miseries— the cars that broke down, the pipes that leaked, the appliances that caught fire, the deepening debt, the man who beat her and then broke down in tears, the son in a juvenile home for some crime Lila wouldn't reveal. Most of the time he hadn't been paying attention, staring down at his plate while Virginia went on and on, he asking himself what a woman like that was doing in their lives.

Once he said to Virginia, "Do you want to replace her? Get someone else?"

Virginia was shocked. "Oh no! She needs me, the work. And I

164

need her. She cleans so well."

Lila came out of the kitchen and moved toward the stairway, arms laden with a broom, a mop, and two buckets.

"Do you want help?" Mason asked her.

"I've been doing this for years. I never need help."

She climbed one step at a time, her back and her rear broad in faded denim, the ends of her pants legs flapping frayed over black work shoes. Her footsteps in the hallway were heavy. Then she dropped everything she had been carrying, a clamor that made him start. Her cleaning continued the noise—splashing, wood banging into wood, a roaring vacuum that she must have retrieved from an upstairs closet.

Mason wondered if she were destroying things, taking revenge for years of having to clean up after people who had so much more, a woman who wore stylish dresses and had easy work in the shop of a close friend. But that woman, for all her comforts, lay in a mortuary, and Lila had survived to repair the mess of her dying.

He sat on the edge of the sofa, his hands folded in his lap, and tried to imagine what she was doing. There hadn't been blood, not that he knew of, but toward the end Virginia had thrown up frequently; he could hear her retching. He didn't smell anything, but perhaps there had been splatters. I should be doing this, he thought, yet he didn't move.

When the noises stopped and Lila came back down, she carried a bulging black trash bag and an armful of balled sheets that she took to the laundry room. Mason could hear the rush of water and then the churning. From the doorway to the kitchen, he could see the sweat glistening on Lila's face, the stains on her shirt across her chest, under her arms.

"I'm sorry you had to do so much," he told her.

"It's what happens when people die. And I'm not done."

"Will you have to come back?"

"Tomorrow. I can't stay here any more now."

Mason remembered the plan. "My children will be here tomorrow."

"I won't bother your children." She shut the door with a slam.

Mason opened a can of food, and had no idea what he was spooning from the bowl to his mouth, tasted nothing. After darkness fell, he went out to the garden. It was a beautiful night. He stood in one place for a long time, looking up at the moon, breathing the scent of the lilac bush as he had done in that yard for so many years, when things were normal. He wanted so much for things to be normal.

He had left no lights on in his house. Its dark shape loomed against the horizon. The windows of the other houses on the block were all bright. He wondered what the people who lived in them thought when they saw the hearse, if the strangers who had never known Virginia shuddered at the death in their midst, if those who did, people she had waved to across the lawns, would feel relief that it was someone else.

Lila's insistent ringing of the chimes awoke Mason in the morning. He had finally fallen into a deep sleep and sat up bewildered, thrashing at the comforter. His slippers weren't at the edge of the bed. He went down barefoot, wrapping a robe around his pajamas. By then he understood who would be standing there when he opened the door. He considered telling her to go home, come back another day, sometime after the funeral. But she pushed inside and headed for the kitchen.

"I was sleeping," he told her.

"You look terrible."

He realized that his sinuses were burning, his throat filled with mucus that he tried to clear with a hacking sound, then ended up coughing.

"You want coffee?"

He nodded. While he stood in the living room, Lila banged cabinets in the kitchen, drawers sliding back and forth, water running, silverware clattering. Everything she did made noise.

The coffeemaker gurgled, the aroma reminding Mason how much he craved it.

"Come in here," Lila said. She had set two mugs on the kitchen table, folded napkins beside them.

As he sat, he remembered this had been Lila's ritual with Virginia once a week when she arrived. Coffee and conversation. He wondered which of them had made it—employer or worker.

He sipped and looked out the window at the birds hovering around the empty feeder. Filling it had been Virginia's task, a hobby. No one had done it for weeks

"Did you consider Virginia a friend?" he asked Lila, still facing toward the window

"She liked to talk to me."

Now he turned to see her face. From Virginia's reports, he assumed she had been the listener, sitting there as a favor to Lila, perhaps with a guilty relief that this woman's life was so much worse than hers. "About what?" he said.

"Her troubles. What was bothering her."

"What kinds of troubles?"

Lila rattled a spoon in her cup, tasted, and rattled again. "If she didn't tell you, I guess she didn't want you to know."

Nonsense, Mason wanted to say but instead asked, "About her illness?"

"She never said anything about that."

Lila stood up quickly and spilled the rest of her coffee in the sink, rinsed the cup. She gathered her cleaning supplies. Arms laden, at the foot of the stairway, she said, "Come up and tell me what to throw out, what to keep."

He shook his head. "You decide." He wouldn't go up. He would seal the door and never enter that guest room again. But as she worked, Lila kept shouting down to him. What about those towels, that nightgown, the bars of soap, the bedpan? And each time he called back, "Throw it out." He went to the garden to escape her questions.

He was sitting in an Adirondack chair when the limo bringing his children from the airport pulled into the drive. They had scheduled flights to arrive at similar times. He heard doors shut, luggage being retrieved, the voice of the driver, and he was hesitant to go to them, unsure what he should say, what they would say.

Finally, with the sound of the limo backing out to the street, he stepped around the side of the house and went to his children. None of them spoke. His son shook his hand. His daughters stood side by side. As much as they sounded alike on the phone, they were striking opposites in person, the one who looked like Virginia long and thin, with the same unruly curls of auburn hair, the other short and plump, her face round and pink. She was the one who stepped forward and hugged him, a brief light embrace. Then her tall sister reached out to squeeze his arm.

He carried his daughters' suitcases and led them inside, placing the luggage against a wall in the hallway. Although their old rooms were available, the same furniture they had grown up with dusted, the beds made by Lila, they had chosen to stay in a hotel. "You've got enough going on without having to fuss with us," his son had said on the phone the day before, and Mason didn't argue.

As the four of them stood uncertainly in the living room, Lila squeezed down the stairs with three bulging black plastic bags. "This is Lila," he told his children. "She's worked for your mother for years." Then he introduced his children by name. They said "hello" and Lila just nodded, edging toward the kitchen door.

"Let me help you with those." Mason took the one that looked heaviest from her, hoping his son wouldn't offer. He didn't want him to have to touch any of the mess. He followed Lila out to the shed at the end of the patio where the garbage cans were stored. She stuffed the three trash bags into a corner.

"Is that everything?" Mason asked.

"Most of it. I'll have to come back another time."

"Of course."

Then he looked at her closely and saw that she had one of Virginia's necklaces around her neck, an elaborate brooch fastened crookedly to her denim shirt, objects from the jewelry box in the master bedroom. The large bags had hidden them.

"What are you doing?" He pointed, turned his index finger in a circle from neck to chest.

"She gave me these."

"When? I never heard anything about it."

She covered her shirt with a forearm, brought the other hand to her throat.

About to shout for his son, Mason changed his mind. Perhaps Virginia had. The pieces couldn't have been worth much. And what if they were? He didn't care. His daughters wouldn't wear them. They weren't to their tastes.

"She wanted me to have them," Lila insisted.

"All right. Take them."

Mason left her in the shed and went back to his children. He expected them to ask about Lila, but no one did. Mason said nothing about the jewelry. His son had questions about their mother's last days. His younger daughter was weeping, softly, dabbing a handkerchief to her eyes. Then they began speaking about good times, when they were young, things their mother did with them, costumes she had made, parties she had arranged. Soon they were laughing, and Mason relaxed.

The next morning at the funeral home, Mason and his children sat in the front close to the draped coffin, some friends scattered among the rows of padded folding chairs, a few old schoolmates of his son and daughters, everyone silent or whispering. Mason heard the squeak of a door at the back of the room. Lila slipped inside and took a chair in the rear. He had never seen her in a dress, this one dark and shapeless, Virginia's necklace glittering red and gold, the brooch pinned below it, still crooked.

He couldn't concentrate on the service, his son's litany of his mother's virtues, the official eulogy, all the time staring at the shiny mahogany of the coffin, lost in the mystery of what was encased within. My life, he kept thinking, and wondered what was left.

Then, suddenly, the service was over, and two black-suited men wheeled the coffin out through a back door. Virginia wanted to be cremated. So did he. They had put that in their wills, directing that no one should be there, no family, no friends, just those whose work it was. He would never see Virginia again.

The funeral director aligned Mason and his children at the front entrance to the room to shake hands and hear the murmured sympathy of those who had attended. His daughters gave faint smiles to each one. His son looked solemn. Mason just nodded.

He realized he was waiting for Lila in the line of people, but she wasn't there. When the room was nearly empty, his children off in a corner talking to friends, he went out to the lawn, seeking light and fresh air.

Lila was waiting on the stone pathway at the base of the steps. Mason felt he had to speak to her.

"Thanks for coming." He reached out to shake her hand as he had done with all the others.

She kept her arms at her side. "I don't like your children."

"You hardly know them." He felt a surge of anger.

"They're cold people. Like their father."

"And Virginia was their mother."

"None of you deserved Virginia!" Lila was crying, and he thought she might start wailing again. Instead she shouted. "You never knew her! I'm mourning for you all!"

Mason realized he had not paid her for her work. He pulled the wallet from his coat pocket and stripped off bills, not looking at them, not counting. He gripped her wrist and pressed the money into her hand.

Mason turned his back and spoke as he walked away, "I'll be getting someone else to clean."

Walter Cummins has published four previous short story collections—*Witness*, *Where We Live*, *Local Music*, and *The End of the Circle*. Another, *Habitat*, is pending. More than 100 of his stories, as well as memoirs, essays, and reviews, have appeared in magazines such as *Kansas Quarterly*, *Virginia Quarterly Review*, *Under the Sun*, *Confrontation*, *Bellevue Literary Review*, *Connecticut Review*, *The Laurel Review*, *Other Voices*, *Georgetown Review*, *Contrary*, *Sonora Review*, *Abiko Quarterly*, *Weber Studies*, *Midwest Quarterly*, *West Branch*, *South Carolina Review*, *Crosscurrents*, *Crescent Review*, *The MacGuffin*, in book collections, and on the Web. He is co-publisher of Serving House Books, an outlet for novels, story collections, poetry, and essays. For more than twenty years, he was editor of *The Literary Review*. He teaches in Fairleigh Dickinson University's MFA in Creative Writing Program.

www.ingramcontent.com/pod-product-compliance
Lightning Source LLC
Chambersburg PA
CBHW051824170626
46807CB00003B/1016